John Aason Mysteries
by John Cain

The Dead Judge Rolled Over

The Dead Judge and the Raid Gone Bad

The Dead Judge and Golden Buddha

The Prosecutor and the Obsidian Knife

The Prosecutor, the Truck, & the Mermaid

The Prosecutor and the Gem Stones

All That the Rain Promised and More

The Curious Death of Silas Smith

A Cup of Malice

The Curious Death of Silas Smith

John Cain

While cosmic wisdom
understands all things
are good and just,
intelligence may find
injustice here, and justice
somewhere else.

-Heracltus

The world's perverse,
but it could be worse.

-Mona Van Duyn

Dedication

For my father, Roger J. Cain

Disclaimer

This is a work of fiction. Any resemblance to the living or the dead or to places is a coincidence and unintended. Harbor City and Hardin County are fictional political entities.

Acknowledgments

As always I owe a great debt to my friend, Barb Immermann, who graciously reads whatever I send to her.

The article, "Why I am an Episcopalian," originally appeared in the Tartan newsletter. The article on Malice and the article on litigants who represent themselves were originally published in the Tacoma Pierce County Bar News. The Creed of Professionalism is the Washington Lawyers Creed of Professionalism with a minor modification. Joy Lorton proofread the original draft. Ann Carlsen read closely the manuscript twice and gave me suggestions. My sister Susannah Cain, and my friends Phil Dantes and Bill Tammaro read drafts of this book and gave me helpful suggestions. Rita Griffith suggested a needed change. Her attention to detail helped many criminal defendants win on appeal. Bill Kelly, a retired English high school teacher, has give me great advice and encouragement. I have had a lot of help and support in writing this book. All errors and typos are my responsibility.

I owe a great debt to my wife, Bobbi Cain without her support and patience this book could not have been written.

A Request for Assistance

William H Roetzheim, editor of the Giant Book of Poetry, requested in the forward to his book that people be tolerant of his errors and that they be brought to his attention so that he could fix them in future printings of his book. I thought that an incredibly humble request and one that is certainly needed by me. Despite the efforts of many friends to catch my errors some pass through. If you find one please bring it to my attention at johnccain@icloud. I will correct for later printings. To my friends who joyfully told me they had found typos, misspellings and other errors in my books but would not tell me where they were screw you, too.

Partial List of Characters

Ashley, the manager of Things, Things & Things
Baily Jarad, a six-year-old child
Billie Abel, John Abel's spouse
Benis Dalton, a real estate agent
Brandy Ryan, a mother of a child
Bryan Steiner, Medical Examiner of Hardin County
David Levi Yabroff, a seaman
Denise Jarad, mother of Randy and Baily
Elizabeth Knight, a Police Sergeant
Father Martin Wojciehowicz
Jeff McDonald, neighbor of the Daltons
Judge Nightingale, a Superior Court Judge
John Abel, a lawyer
Jeffery Adams, an advocate for the homeless
Laconia Jones, a homicide sergeant
Linda Garvey, a custodian of minor children
Lori Black, an in-home caregiver
Mandy Ryan, twin of Brandy Ryan
Marsha Barnes, a former ward of Linda Garvey
Michael Rosekrans, a Public Defender
Mr. Jones, a photographer
Randy Jarad, a nine-year-old child
Rob Washington, a friend of Sean Riley
Roberta Jarad, grandmother of Randy and Baily
Robert Culpepper, a court-appointed Investigator
Ron McBride, a friend of John Abel
Sally Grimes, a waitress
Samual Blount, a lawyer
Sean Riley, a homeless veteran
Sheri Dalton, wife of Benis Dalton
Silas Smith, a resident of Harbor City

1

Benis Dalton was angry. All he wanted was a parking space but none were right for him. There was an opening near Bob's Barbecue, but a grill was set up in front of the place, and billows of smoke and the scent of barbecue were in the air. He didn't want his BMW smelling of barbecue and rushed away from the spot, giving the cook an angry stare. Even when he was most satisfied with himself, he was an angry man. This morning he'd gotten some measure of revenge on a man, but he was not certain if the man would know it was him who had caused the grief. If the man didn't know it was him, was it worth the risks he had taken? If he ever thought he was losing his undercurrent of anger, he brought it back with thoughts of past slights, injustices, insults, and honors that were never fairly given to him. He considered anger the edge that made him a winner in all things that mattered.

He turned a corner and saw a spot. He had hoped to keep his car on a main street, but there were no open spots available. He was in the Center Point district of Harbor City. Not the best part of town if you were white and it was after dark. But it was noontime and he had nothing of value in his car. His sports jacket and laptop were in the trunk. When he got close, he saw it was a handicap parking spot, but he pulled into it anyway.

The spot was in front of a two-story frame house with an AA sign on the front. A few men and women were chatting and taking last drags on their cigarettes before the noon meeting began. Most of the loiterers were men, but there were a few women as well. He recognized the lawyer John Abel standing next to a large Black man. He knew Abel from a criminal case. Dalton had been assaulted by a dumpy Polack who pulled a gun on him. Abel had somehow gotten the case dismissed. Just another example of how the system was geared to help Whites and put down Blacks as far as he was concerned.

Dalton stepped out of his car, and the large Black man talking to Abel called out that he had to move his car. "Can't park there. That's a handicap spot." The large man had a raspy voice like he smoked five packs of cigarettes a day, followed by an equal number of daily jabs to his throat. Dalton sized him up as big but slow, someone he could bounce jabs off like he had the Polack.

"Give me a break, bro."

"I am not your bro. My brothers don't wear gray slacks with pink shirts. You need to move the car."

"I'll just be a minute. I want to grab some soup from the Vietnamese place a street over."

"There's a lady who wants to park where you are, and she has a handicap sticker," said Abel, pointing to an older Cadillac that was waiting for the spot.

"Abel, you can't make me move. Call a cop and see if anyone gives me a ticket!" Dalton shouted. "You can't make me move."

From behind the large Black man another man appeared with a screwdriver. "You've been asked nicely to move your car. This is a nice neighborhood, but bad things can happen to fancy cars with nice paint jobs." The man ran his hand with the point of the screwdriver just an inch above the hood of the car. "McBride and Mr. John asked you nicely to move your car. You should move your car." The man's smile was filled with gold crowns.

Dalton said to Abel, "I should have known you were a drunk."

"Pity you aren't," said Abel. "There might be some hope for you."

Making sure that they saw him shaking his head and rolling his eyes, Dalton retreated from the parking space.

At Eleventh Street he turned right and moved into the center lane as he passed the barbecue smoker. At Frederick Douglass Boulevard he turned right. At the corner was the Vietnamese restaurant where he had wanted to get takeout. Half a block down a parking space had opened up. He parked in front of a local clothing store that carried low priced shirts and colorful suits of bright yellow and purple. It also sold matching hats favored by a local man who preached the gospel in the halls of the local mall near Dalton's real estate office. Dalton thought him an embarrassment, but security guards thought him harmless. He called in a take-out order of noodle soup and spring rolls, then made a couple of phone calls. The first was to his office to grill the receptionist about any calls she might not have forwarded to him. He was certain she favored the white brokers over him in the office. Twice she assured him that no one had called for him. Then he called his afternoon appointment to confirm that they were still on. Like a fine-tuned race car he went from condescending to ubiquitous in an instant. He assured the client that a half hour later start time was no problem at all, and he was there to serve them.

With his lunch in a paper sack, he walked two short blocks to the People's Park. On the meridian across from the park were several homeless tents with black garbage bags off to the side. Weeks ago the Harbor City Police Department and Social Services had cleared out the park. Like weeds, they were already returning from wherever they had been displaced.

The People's Park was a three-block square of mainly open space. The trees that were once in the area had been cut down then as an afterthought, it was decided to turn the unused land into a city park. In the heart of the

People's Park was a recreational area with two basketball hoops separated by a play section with a Big Toy. Along the sides of the space were picnic tables and benches. Most of the picnic tables were unoccupied. He chose one near the Big Toy and opened his sack. He had asked the bitch for extra packets of salt, pepper, and soy sauce, but they weren't in the bag, nor were the extra napkins he'd requested. But the soup was good, and he was given an extra packet of chili sauce for the spring rolls.

On the far side of the Big Toy were a couple of mothers with baby carriages while their slightly older kids played nearby. In the center was a wide slide with steps leading up to it. Back and forth two boys chased each other. They appeared to be about nine and six, and they were not white or Black, but some mixture of South Asian, Indian or Samoan. They intrigued him for many reasons. There were no parents or adults who appeared to be related to them. He bit into a spring roll and took a sip of cold tea from a can. No sooner had the larger of the two boys landed at the bottom than the smaller one came laughing after him. The older one caught him at the bottom, then raced off to the steps with the smaller one yelling and laughing after him. As the boys raced about, he scanned the park for whoever was watching them.

On the same side of the picnic table, a middle aged very dark skinned Black woman sat down. She was overweight, with ponderous breasts. She had shiny black hair pressed into waves. She put a tote bag down on the bench seat between them. "They are with me," she said.

"Who?"

"The two boys," she said. "I saw you scanning the park."

"What of it? I was worried that they might not have supervision."

"This is the third day in a row you have come here to watch the boys."

"What of it?"

"No need to be defensive and all. I just noticed that you were here before. I am the custodian of those boys."

"I like the park. Lots of activity to watch." He nodded toward the basketball courts.

"Every time you've been here you've sat down at this table across from the Big Toy."

"It is centrally located. I can see the activity in both courts this way."

"What are you, a lawyer, a doctor?"

"I sell real estate all over the state."

"Wherever you go, you're just a Black man in fancy clothes."

"My mother was a white Jew. I was raised Jewish."

"All that means is that no matter where you go, you're not welcome. Why are you here?"

"I like the soup."

"Uh huh." The woman nodded her disbelief. "Those are nice young boys. I have trained them well. They do what I tell them. My name is Linda Garvey. You should call me." She smiled and licked her thick lips. "I can write down my number for you—"

"What are you doing, Linda?" demanded a man, blocking Dalton's view of the Big Toy. He was late middle age or early senior status with short gray hair and a close cropped goatee. He wore a dark purple suit and matching derby with a white band.

"Silas, I'm just talking to the man. Besides, we have no agreement."

"I know you. You promised me."

"I promised you nothing, and you've given me nothing," shot back the woman.

13

"What did she promise you?" he yelled at Dalton as he slammed the heel of his hand on the picnic table, making the bowl of soup bounce.

"Nothing, she promised me nothing!" yelled Dalton back. Rising up, he came around the picnic table.

"I have seen you eyeing the boys!" shouted Silas.

"I am not that kind."

"Bullshit," said Silas, jabbing a finger into Dalton's chest. Quickly Dalton landed a right to the man's temple, then he moved slightly to the left and landed a second blow under the man's eye. He bounced back and landed another right into the man's jaw, sending him to the ground as if hit with a butcher's hammer.

Dalton stood over the man who had crumpled onto the ground in the fetal position while covering his head. Not far from him his derby landed upside down.

"Stop!" yelled Linda.

"He attacked me! He attacked me!"

"He's a preacher. You'd best go," said the woman. Two women across the lot were picking up their cell phones and pointing at Dalton.

"I defended myself."

"He's an old preacher, and you're a young buck with not a mark on you. You'd best go. I'll cover for you. The police won't know who you are or where to look. Go."

Dalton backed away, sprinting out of the park. Then he slowed his pace down when a patrol car passed by with the officer giving him a hard stare. Afraid to look over his shoulder, he kept his head down and made it to his car. He was unsure if the police were looking for him, and he cursed his decision to run away. Nothing a white cop likes more than humiliating a Black person except humiliating a Black man dressed in fine clothes

14

2

Linda helped Silas to his feet and guided him to the picnic table to sit down. As she guided him, she brushed off the back of his suit coat covered in playground dust and twigs. "Brother Silas, are you all right?" she asked several times.

"We saw what happened," said one of the women who had been videoing what happened. She was in her twenties and pushing a baby carriage. Next to her was another woman. They looked like twins and were dressed like twins. Each was wearing tight designer jeans with lots of thigh spread, sports bras under their blue shirts, and gold hoop earrings. They had milk chocolate complexions with hints of blush on their prominent cheekbones. They were at the park at midday but dressed like they had plans for the evening.

"We saw it all," they both said at the same time. "Should we call the police?"

"Brother Silas, how are you?" asked Linda.

"Where is he?" muttered Silas.

"He ran off," said one of the women. "But we videoed what happened. The police can find him." She held up her cell phone and shook it back and forth. "He can be found."

"Brother Silas, do you want that? Do you want to have another young Black man hauled into court? You did provoke him."

"I provoked him with the truth," snapped back Silas.

"Your truth," said Linda. "Who can look into the heart of man? Not even Jesus condemned the woman who the village wanted to stone. Vengeance is the Lord's. To each other we should be in all things compassionate."

"That man attacked Brother Silas," said the woman with the baby carriage.

"Didn't you see Brother Silas slam his hand down on the table?" asked Linda.

The two young women nodded in unison, and then the one without a child said, "But all he did was put his hand on the picnic table. I didn't hear him slamming his hand down."

"I did and I was close by. You were far away. I was afraid that Brother Silas was going to put his hands on the young man."

"I would never do such a thing."

"I know that, but did the young man?" asked Linda. "You didn't even know him, and you accused him of a terrible thing."

"I did accuse him of an awful thing," said Silas.

"Yes, you did. All he was doing was sitting at a picnic table having lunch in a public park. Is that what you want? To put another Black man in jail or tarnish him for life with an assault charge?"

"That man hit Brother Silas hard. He hit him several times," said the woman with the cell phone. "I have it here. Young children should not have to see that," she said and motioned to the two small children who had huddled next to Linda. The older one was pressed against Linda's side, and the smaller one was trying to crawl into her lap.

Linda pulled the smaller child into her lap and kissed the older one on the forehead.

"I don't want these young children hauled into court. No matter what they saw I don't want them being hauled into court," said Linda.

"No, that would not be good," said Silas.

Silas started to stand up, then sat back down again with a hand on the table to steady himself.

16

"How are you, Brother Silas?" asked the woman with the baby carriage. "You seem kind of woozy." Holding up two fingers, she asked how many fingers Silas could see.

"Well, aren't you the little playground nurse wannabe? Holding up two fingers and acting all official," said Linda.

"He rung my bell a bit, but I'll be fine," said Silas, puffing his chest out a bit. "I have been hit by better men than him, that's for sure. I used to train at the Les Davis Boys' Club. That was back in the day when boxers from Harbor City won gold at the Olympics."

"My grandpa told me about those days," said the woman without a child. "That was some time ago. You should go to the emergency room and get checked out. Did you lose consciousness, and are you having trouble seeing things?"

"Are you a doctor or a nurse?" snapped Linda. "If he says he's all right, then he's all right."

"I'm fine," smiled Silas. "The Lord was looking out for me."

"I'll sit with him for awhile," said Linda. "You two don't have to stay." Picking up the derby hat, she began to carefully brush dust away from the brim and set it on the table. The two women wished him well and walked away.

"If you begin to feel nauseous or you get a headache, you should go to the doctor."

"I will be fine," said Silas. "I just need to catch my breath."

After the two women were out of earshot, Linda shooed the two boys back to the Big Toy slide and leaned in close to Silas. "It wasn't just the young man that you

17

spoke evil of. You said harsh things about me as well. Why was that? Silas, I have never harmed you."

"I have known you since you were a child. Why are you with those children?"

"I take care of them. I am their custodian."

"I have never known you to look out for anyone but yourself."

"What a terrible thing to say, Brother Silas." Linda shook her head in disbelief.

"It is who you are. I remember you sneaking off from choir to smoke cigarettes and do whatever you wanted when you were supposed to be singing the praises of the Lord."

She helped him onto the picnic bench and brushed some more dirt from his suit coat. "I have changed some. The mother of the two boys does cleaning and cooking for me. But she is slow-witted. She gave me custody, and I take care of the boys. She can't manage money and was getting fifteen hundred dollars a month for each boy. She just couldn't handle the finances and the responsibility of the boys," she confided.

"So you are making money off them. I knew it."

"I get Section 8 housing assistance because they live with me."

"That is the Linda I know," pronounced Silas.

"I've been bad, I know it. But I've changed. They have good hot meals, and I provide for them."

"I know some of the people you associate with. Drug dealers and thieves. Maybe worse. Center Point has many levels, and you have always been at the bottom."

"That is just harsh, Brother Silas. If it was not for your age and the respect I have for you, I would regret stopping that young man from attacking you."

"I do thank you for that. Are you sure it wasn't for fear of the police coming?"

"Come to my house tonight for dinner. You can see the boys in their home, meet their mother and make up your own mind about whether I am treating them properly or not."

Brother Silas stroked his chin and scratched his head in thought. "Just like that you would invite me over to see your place?"

"Yes, indeed, When you see how well I treat them you can tell whoever you want how I treat them and how their mother is glad I've saved them from the life they were living."

"I will come at six. Do you live where you always have?"

"No. Section 8 housing has helped me."

She gave him her new address, and he walked away, waving at the boys who smiled and waved back at him from the top of the Big Toy slide. After he reached the edge of the park, Linda telephoned Denise Jarad, the mother of Randy and Baily.

"I need you to come over today to clean the house and fix dinner."

"I was coming tomorrow to see the boys and take them for ice cream."

"You can come tomorrow as well. But I need you at my house today. I need the house spotless, and you can stay for dinner."

"Just like a family."

"Just like a family with an honored guest, Brother Silas."

"Who?"

"The Black man who dresses in bright suits and walks around the mall talking to anyone who is fool enough to listen to him."

"I know who that is."

"Well, he is coming for dinner, and I want him leaving happy and satisfied that the boys living with me is the best thing for them."

"When can they come live with me again? You said it would only be for a month or two, and it has been a year."

"When I say so. That's when they can come live with you. You see them when you want to now."

"Not like I used to."

"You will see them even less if you don't appreciate me and all I have done for you."

"I'm sorry. Don't be angry with me."

Linda broke the connection without saying another word.

"Get your asses over here," she barked at the boys. They immediately froze at the sound of her voice and then raced over to her. When they reached her she said, "We are going on a scavenger hunt for free food. You know what that means?"

The boys nodded.

"That means we don't scavenger hunt near where we live," said Randy, the older boy. He was nine years old

"What are the rules of a scavenger hunt?"

"Don't get caught," said Randy.

"And if you're caught, cry and say you're sorry and never ever snitch on you or my brother," said Baily, the younger boy. He was six years old.

"That's right," answered Linda. "You both make me proud. Pay attention to me and when I want a distraction, make one."

When they got to her car, she gave them both a long sleeve loose fitting shirt she called scavenger shirts to wear over the shirts they had on. She buttoned the top button of her dress, then put a scarf over her head. She put on a raincoat that had extra deep inside pockets she had sewn into it. She drove out of the Center Point district of Harbor City to the small shopping area in the north end of the city. In the area were several retail shops specializing in used books and upscale but affordable dresses. There was also a movie theater that ran old movies or recent movies no longer shown at the newest theaters with big screens and easy chairs. Also, two large supermarkets across from one another were featured. One was a Safeway that specialized in inferior produce near the expiration dates, plus low priced meats all marked at near cost. There was a Thriftway with a bakery, an espresso stand, a cheese and meat deli, and high end organic meats, fruits, and vegetables. Because the district was a mixture of working class and professionals, the parking lots of both supermarkets were always full.

Linda pulled into an angular stall in the Thriftway parking lot and warned the two boys that if either got caught, they would both be whipped with a coat hanger. With eyes wide open and deep swallows, the boys nodded that they understood what was expected of them.

Linda took a large shopping cart from its rack and put two canvas shopping bags in it. She displayed them in the small front portion of the cart. *Always best to look like a loyal return customer*, thought Linda. As they walked in, a security guard stared at her, and she smiled back at him.

Near the front of the store, at the cheese and meat deli she got two different types of hard cheese, one soft cheese, one pound of Genoa salami cured, and one pound of uncured Genoa salami. Moving on, she put lettuce, potatoes and carrots in her basket. When she was near the display of tomatoes, she slipped one of the cheeses and one of the salamis into the inner pocket of her coat.

Near the meat section of the store, she motioned for the boys to start pushing and shoving each other. While they created a distraction, she put a whole chicken in her basket and another whole chicken under her coat. At the checkout line each boy reached for three chocolate bars. She slapped their hands and they replaced two bars each, keeping one tucked under a sleeve in the hollow of their hands just as she had taught them.

On the way home they laughed and celebrated with the sodas from the lower shelves that the boys had also pilfered.

3

Linda Garvey's rental was a two-story frame house with brick steps leading up to the main door. It was on a side street off of South Twenty-third Street. Among law enforcement, the street was known as the home base of a subdivision of the local Crips gang. To be a member of the gang, one must live near the street and have a tattoo referencing the street. Members most often also had a tattoo of a pair of dice on their forearms with two and three dots right side up. Linda had lived in the area most of her life in one Section 8 house or another. Those living on the street were considered criminals who sported their criminal affiliations as nothing more than inmates in waiting.

Linda's house was one of the better Section 8 houses with three bedrooms and a freestanding garage in the back. But when she saw a woman sitting on the front steps, Linda decided to park in front of the house and confront the woman, rather than giving her a chance to run off. She parked behind an older model car with faded paint and highlighted with a few dents. The woman was white, but not dressed well enough to be a social worker. Linda guessed that she might be a junkie looking for a fix. This was not a part of town where white women simply sat around without the protection of a pimp.

"Bring the bags but stay behind me," Linda admonished the boys as she lumbered up the front walk. Catching her breath, she demanded, "Who are you and why are you here?"

The woman stood up and introduced herself, "I'm Lori Black."

She was a slender woman of moderate height with very black hair and pale skin. She wore little makeup, and although she was thin, she was not junkie thin. She was wearing worn blue jeans and an old sweater with J.C. Penny brand labels on them.

"Lori Black, why are you on my steps?"

The curious boys peeked out from behind Linda.

"I was waiting for you. I was appointed as your new caregiver. The Korean Women's Association sent me. They told me to be here at 1:00 p.m. I've been waiting an hour. Didn't they tell you I was coming?"

"I thought it was tomorrow."

"We were scavenger hunting," volunteered the older boy, Randy. "We…"

Linda shot him a look, and he became as mute as a pillar of salt. Who needs a whip when a stare will do?

"I have the letter from the agency. It was mailed to you as well."

"I get a lot of mail," sneered Linda. "Come in and start cleaning. I want the place looking extra good. I have a guest coming to dinner tonight. I want this place extra clean not white girl clean."

The Korean Association like Catholic Services administered some state money to those in need. It was a private organization that relieved the state of some administrative costs. People who contracted with it did not have to be paid at the higher rate that state employees received. The administrator who Lori reported to had warned her that Garvey could be difficult, but even so she had not expected the abuse she was receiving right out of the gate. Lori took a deep breath, remembered she needed the job and said, "I have to leave by 4:00 to pick up my son from school."

"You have a son? You'll have to bring him over. I love children," said Linda, hugging the younger boy close to her.

"The association said you need a person to clean, run errands, and do some cooking for you."

"I don't like white girls cooking for me. The food never tastes good."

"I've have never gotten complaints before. Part of my job duties entail shopping for you and cooking."

"You haven't worked for me before. Whatever I tell you to do *are* your job duties." Linda then shook her head, smiled a toothy smile and added, "Tonight their mother is coming over to cook. I need the place spotless so you should get to work. I need the place white glove spotless."

Once inside, Lori saw that her skills were needed and asked where the supplies were kept. On a table next to a pile of monthly *Glamor* magazines she saw the letter from the Korean Woman's Association stating she was the new caregiver. It was next to several some other letters and documents strewn on the table partially covering one another. The letter stated that Linda had been awarded an additional twenty-five hours of service a month because of her obesity, diabetes, and heart condition. Yet another document from Social Security approved her for another year as caregiver for the two boys with a cost of living increase. How a woman who could not take care of herself was expected to raise two young boys baffled Lori, but she needed the money. So she thought it best not to ask. While Lori dusted, polished, and scrubbed, Linda sat in a large easy chair playing patty cake with the younger boy. The older boy sat on the floor with his nose facing against a wall as discipline for speaking out of turn and saying they'd been on a scavenger hunt.

As Lori was leaving, she met the mother of the two boys carrying two plastic bags of groceries. She was a heavyset younger woman with dark skin and the features of a Pacific Islander. Garvey introduced them. "This is

Denise. She is the mother of Randy and Baily," she said. "You will see her from time to time."

"I thought once I moved in, you wouldn't need a helper," remarked Denise.

"After you move in, we'll cross that bridge," Linda replied. "But you're not ready to move in right now. You need to learn a few things."

"What things?"

"Things," said Linda. "How to take better care of the boys. Did you bring the collards and bacon?"

Denise nodded that she had.

"There are two chickens in the kitchen. You need to burn off the pinfeathers and get them in the oven. We have a guest tonight. An important guest. "Did you bring the baked potatoes and sour cream?"

"Yes. Here's the grocery receipt. I got the collards, bacon, onion, and pinto beans just like you told me to," Denise said, holding it out in her hand.

"What's that for? You're eating here tonight, aren't you?"

"Yes, but you get Social Security money for the boys."

"I don't get money for feeding you or the guests I bring into the house. I paid for the chicken, broth, rice, ice cream, and peach cobbler that comes with the meal. You need to contribute too. After all I've done for you, you still think you have the right to complain!" snapped Linda, wagging her finger at Denise's nose. "Now, get to those pinfeathers," she admonished, pointing to the kitchen. "After the chicken is in the oven, the boys need to take a bath. If you were better trained, you'd know that. You need to know these things without me telling you."

By the time Silas arrived, the dining room table was set, and the boys were clean with their hair slicked back from their bathwater. Linda saw no need to waste good shampoo on boys who would just get dirty again.

"Silas, so glad you are here," Linda cooed as she ushered him into the front room. "How are you? Recovered from your beating?" she asked as she seated him in her favorite easy chair. Not waiting for a reply, she asked Silas what he wanted to drink.

"Just water."

"The drink of John the Baptist," smiled Linda, ordering Denise to fetch a glass of water with ice from the kitchen.

"So, how is it that you have become the caregiver for these boys?"

"Denise is their mother, and their father is dead. He killed himself. Denise was overwhelmed with grief and the obligations of raising the boys. She was doing house cleaning for a man and had trouble managing her money. I stepped in to help her manage her money and the boys."

"Is that right?" Silas asked Denise. "You gave up your children to this woman?"

"It's just temporary, no matter what the court papers say," responded Denise. "Until I get on my feet and settled. I'm going to move in here soon. Isn't that right?" she said, looking at Linda who nodded back.

"When you are ready," Linda said softly. "When I say you are ready."

"Court papers?" said Silas.

"We needed to make things official so the Social Security money would come to me," said Linda. "Because of the father's death they qualified for assistance, but Denise just didn't know how to handle the money or the boys."

"That's right," chimed in Denise after a sideways glance from Linda.

"What sort of things is Linda teaching you?"

"Discipline. I have been far too easy on the boys. I have spoiled them."

"Discipline?" mused Silas.

"Spare the rod and spoil the child. Colored kids need discipline," said Linda. "Without it they will talk back to the wrong person, and you know how that can end."

"Those lesbian bitches from Child Protective Services have no idea how to raise a Black child," piped up Randy.

"Is that right?" Silas queried.

"That is what Mama Linda says," said Randy with a big smile.

"Kids hear things," said Linda, "and repeat the things they should not."

"I'm sorry," said Randy. "I'm sorry."

"You are fine," said Linda. "You just forgot yourself and place for a moment."

"Yes, you are fine," said Denise.

But Randy's distress, manifested with him pacing back and forth uncontrollably, told Silas that all was not fine. "Has CPS been to see you, Linda?"He asked.

"A teacher complained to CPS a while back. The boys are seeing a counselor now, and all is good," reassured Linda. "They have anger issues from the death of their father. He killed himself in his car while they were playing nearby."

"Why did a teacher complain?"

"Randy and Baily had minor marks on their legs, hardly noticeable. They were playing hard, and it looked like they were struck with an electric cord or a clothes hanger. It has all been resolved, though. The boys explained that they were playing with a clothesline they found in a drawer. Isn't that right boys?" Linda said, raising her voice.

"Yes, Mama Linda," the boys said at the same time.

"What did I tell you about eavesdropping on grown-up talk?"

"Not to do it," they both said, shaking their heads.

"That's right, but I forgive you," Linda smirked with a serpentine smile.

At the sound of a timer, Linda announced that it was time for dinner. "Chicken, baked potatoes, collards with bacon, pinto beans and rice, followed by peach cobbler with ice cream for dessert," announced Linda.

After they were seated, Denise brought the serving dishes to the table. Linda sat at the head of the table; Silas sat on opposite; the two boys sat on one side; and Denise sat on the other side. Dinner rolls in a basket covered with a red and white tablecloth were the last to arrive.

As Randy was reaching for one plate and Baily for another, Linda commanded that they wait. Then she added in a voice as sweet as brown sugar, "Brother Silas, will you do us the honor of grace? I don't know why they forgot that we always say grace before we eat."

Silas stretched out his hands, and they all joined hands. Silas bowed his head and said, "Bless us Lord and these gifts that you have bestowed upon us. May we find peace and love in our hearts, be ever grateful for the lives we have been given, and praise the Lord forever and ever. Amen."

While they ate, Linda urged Silas to eat more and more. But he said that while the food was delicious, he wasn't very hungry. He said that since he had been in the park, he had suffered from headaches that came and went.

"You do so much for the community, you should take some time out for yourself and rest more. I know that I have to take breaks occasionally. These boys are a handful, but I tell myself that they are God's gift to me. No matter how much they seem like a cross I am bearing from time to time."

"I am sorry for all the work you do for us," said Denise.

"It is a labor of love." Linda smiled weakly. She seemed to force the smile from her lips.

As he was getting ready to leave, Silas sat down on the easy chair and motioned for the boys to come over to him. "I have red licorice for them, if that is permissible."

"Of course," said Linda.

While the boys were standing next to him, Silas grabbed onto their hands and said, "Let me see those marks that were hardly worth mentioning."

"No need for that!" shouted Linda. "Come here, boys."

Baily's small hand twisted out of Silas' grasp, but he held onto the older boy's hand. Raising Randy's pant leg, he observed three deep red stripes across the boy's calf. Both boys pulled away and ran behind Linda.

"Those are fresh wounds."

"Disciplne was needed. I caught him shoplifting," Linda explained.

"What was the name of that social worker?"

"I forget," said Linda coyly. "This is none of your business."

"I think it is, Linda. I think it is," said Silas as he walked out the door.

"Look what you've done!" Linda shouted at Randy. "You let him hold onto you. You are a spiteful child. Face the wall!"

Silently Randy walked toward the wall and sat down with his nose an inch away from the wall.

"He meant no harm," offered Denise timidly.

"You ungrateful, pathetic loser. There was too much lard on the collards. That is why Silas couldn't eat them. Go clean up the kitchen!" ordered Linda. "I need to talk to Silas. If he calls CPS, you will never see the children again!" She slammed the door on her way out.

4

Silas awoke later than he usually did. He could tell by the slant of the sun rays on the far bedroom wall that it was past nine. He wondered why Evelyn had let him sleep in so late and then remembered that she had passed on several years ago. He propped himself up slowly on his elbows and then laid back down again. The base of his skull throbbed with a dull ache. He waited for it to pass. He glanced about the room. His suit coat laid crumpled up on a chair with the suit pants on top of it where he had left them before tumbling into bed. If Evelyn were alive, there would have been hell to pay for such untidiness. He shook his head at the desire to see her one more time. He went out to the freezer and got an ice pack. Then he laid down again with the blue ice pack at the base of his neck. He dozed off for another hour thinking of the first time he saw her.

It was a warm summer night in Annapolis, Maryland. He was on his way to a pool hall when he saw her walking into a revival meeting. She wore white gloves and a light summer dress that swayed with her hips. Her laugh floated in the air like sweet perfume. Two white boys followed her into the meeting, and he followed them all in. He sat behind the two white boys. He thought if they got out of hand, he would take them down. He heard them talking. They were polite hicks from Iowa who meant no harm.

She walked to the front and stood to the side with two other women as the preacher led the congregation. From time to time they clapped their hands and praised the Lord. On the other side of the preacher was an organist and a man with an electric guitar. After a while, the preacher called for those who were saved to come forward. A few did and a couple of them when stroke on thee foreheads collapsed in ecstasy collapsed. Fortunately strong men were being them to catch them. The preacher came down from the pulpit and confronted the two white boys, and he demanded to know if they were saved. One of the boys said that he was, and the other was silent. Neither came forward to be blessed, but he did. He followed the preacher and stood before a man who struck his forehead. He stared into the eyes of the woman wearing the white gloves and fell backwards into the arms of a man with an iron grip. It was the woman's father. After that day, he kept coming back repeatedly until one day she caught up with him after a service. She told him that he had been saved enough for one century and asked him if he'd like to have a soda with her. He had feigned the ability to speak in tongues for months, but he was suddenly unable to speak until she took his hand and walked him across the street to the corner ice cream parlor.

While they split a double chocolate malt, she told him that she was studying nursing at the Anne Arundel Community College. She told him of her plans to transfer in the fall to a school in the Northwest to get her RN Degree. She wanted a change from the Baltimore area. She had seen too many friends die of drugs or related gunshot wounds. He said that he liked the Northwest and had friends in Dayton, Ohio. She explained that she was headed to the Pacific Northwest, and he said that he could make friends there if given a chance. He was in the Navy but soon to be released. He was a cook at the Naval Academy and due for a promotion if he reenlisted. A commander favored him for his ability to sear a steak and leave the center cold. She said her father would adore him for that talent. They were married before the move to the Northwest. He trained as a welder, and worked at a Navy shipyard. That was where he got the nickname of Slick for his ability to slip into tight corners and cramped spaces where others could not. He stayed in the Naval Reserve until he had put in his thirty years. They had four children: two boys and two girls. None of them lived nearby, but all were doing well. He had his Social Security, Naval pension, and shipyard pension. She had her pension from the hospital plus Social Security. Their house was paid off, and they had money in the bank.

In August the cancer came. By December she was dead. "Don't be bitter my sweetie," she had said gripping his hand with what strength she had left. "Now you will have to know the Lord on your own and not through me. I love you." Those were her last words to him.

How had she known all those years that his faith was merely a reflection of her faith? They had gone regularly to church, including Sunday services and on holidays. When she said they would tithe, he never complained that they could save money or go on a trip instead. He gave willingly because that was what she wanted.

"For God so loved the world, that he gave his only begotten Son, that whosoever believeth in him should not perish, but have everlasting life." This is how much God loved the world. He gave his Son, his one and only Son. He had read that scripture, John 3:16, many times, and each time he read it, he wondered if believing in his wife's faith would be enough. He hoped so, then one night while on his knees praying for faith, he suddenly no longer felt alone. He knew what he could do with the rest of his days. He went past the local men's clothing store and ordered colorful suits, yellow, red, purple, and blue, with matching derby hats. He walked the streets and the shopping centers with a Bible and spoke to all who would listen to him. That was his calling: to simply believe and be available to others who wanted to hear his words.

He got up, showered, made coffee, grits with fried eggs and toast, and read the scripture for the day from a bible that was sectioned into daily readings. When Eve was alive, they read to one another. Now he read the passages to himself in silence. He drank another cup of coffee and tried to remember what had happened after he left Linda's house the night before. His suit was dusty on the back as if he had fallen down, and there was a tear at the kneecap of his pants. He did not remember falling down. He took some aspirin and washed the pills down with water, turned on his computer, and searched for the phone number of the CPS hotline.

He was put in a phone queue and waited his turn while classical music played in his ear. Finally there was a click followed by the message that all calls were confidential and recorded. The identity of the person calling would not be revealed unless by court order, and only after the person had an opportunity to contest the divulging of his or her name. If he agreed to these conditions, he was instructed to say or press the number 1. If he did not, then he was instructed to press or say 2, and hang up. If he pressed or said 1, then he was to stay on the line, and an operator would soon be with him. He pressed 1 and waited. As he waited, the back of his head began to pound, and he put some ice on the back of his neck.

"This is Daily Identification Number 117. To whom am I speaking?" The voice sounded young. Silas gave his name, and in response to the questions, his address, phone number, the name and address of the person he was calling about, the names and ages of the children, and if he had complained about the person or treatment of the children before.

"This is the number I have assigned to your complaint," the voice said and gave him a number. "If you need to call back please include this number."

"Now can I tell you why I called?" Silas demanded.

"Of course," said the voice and added, "Of course, but it is necessary that I have this information and that I get it at the beginning of your call."

"She is beating the kids. I am sure of it."

"Why is that?"

"I don't know why she is beating them. She is a mean greedy person. She always has been. I remember when she stole my daughter's lunch money. She is like a fine steak. Seared nice on the outside but cold and heartless in the center. You think you might be getting a well-cooked steak or one that is medium rare. You cannot tell from the outside, but she is cold inside. Always has been. She is not what she appears to be. She stole from my kids and lied about it when caught."

"When was this?"

"Years ago."

"I am not following you, sir. What I mean is how do you know she is beating the children. Was this years ago?"

"No, not my children. The children she has now, but they are not her children. I don't know how she got a hold of them."

"Did you see her beat the children?"

"No, but she beat them with a cord of some kind."

"How do you know that?"

"I know marks from electric cords."

"Have you beaten children with an electric cord?"

"Of course not, but I know she did."

"But how do you know that, sir?"

"I saw the marks. They were across the children's legs. Deep red welts. Almost purple in color."

"How long ago was this? When did you see them?"

"Yesterday at dinner," said Silas.

"So she feeds them?"

"Yes."

"Is the house clean?"

"Yes, very clean. It is the beating I am calling about. You need to send someone out to investigate. Somehow she got custody of the children."

"You are not the father of the children, are you?"

"No, of course not," said Silas. "She invited me over to see her home."

"Is it a clean home?"

"Very clean."

"And the children are well fed?"

"They look well fed. We had collards and chicken with rice and beans."

"That sounds like a fine meal."

"We had peach cobbler for dessert with vanilla ice cream."

"Doesn't sound like they are in immediate danger," said the voice.

"The children are in danger. I saw the fear in their eyes." His head was pounding and he rubbed his eyes that were starting to water.

"Fear, you say?" the voice repeated with obvious skepticism. "What did this fear look like?"

"Watchfulness. Like they were afraid to say anything she would disapprove of."

"Sounds like she is a disciplinarian teaching them manners."

"Disciplinarians don't use electric cords and leave red welts. They were almost purple."

"You have known Linda Garvey for years? Since your children were young?"

37

"Yes, she is a terrible person. She stole money from my youngest and then looked me in the eye and lied. She is an experienced liar."

"This seems like a long time to wait before lodging a complaint. Have you been thinking about this for some time?"

"This is not about my daughter's lunch money. That was long ago."

"And yet you mentioned it."

"Just to tell you how I know her."

"Did they have marks on their faces?"

"No, none," Silas said, then after a slight hesitation he added, "She is too smart for that."

"Are you sure they just didn't run into something? Boys will be boys. Are you sure they didn't get marks from rough play?"

"I was not there. But I feel it in my bones."

"Hard for us to devote time to a third party's feeling in their bones," drawled the voice.

"But you will investigate?"

"We will investigate your current complaint," assured the speaker. "In due time."

Silas slammed the receiver down, and it sent a shock wave through his arm to the back of his head. He knew, he just knew that nothing would be done, and he resolved to speak to the CPS voice's supervisor.

He splashed some water on his face and the back of his neck. Stepping onto a slippery shower floor seemed like a risky business. He dressed slowly and carefully so as not to lower his head. He chose his red suit and red hat with a white band. The CPS office was on the bus line that led to the Harbor City Mall, and he planned on going there next. There he would walk the halls, speak with those who would speak to him, eat a gyro sandwich, and return home. Eve had disapproved of the Greek gyros at the mall. She thought they slathered too much yogurt on, but he liked the way they made them. He enjoyed the bus ride as an opportunity to read the word of the faith he had been blessed to receive. He had a new family Cadillac Escalade in the garage, but he seldom drove it. Eve had said it was a nice car for putting on airs on Sunday mornings. But on the whole, she preferred the bus where she could talk to people and save money. Now that she was gone, it seemed disloyal to her memory to needlessly drive the Cadillac. Especially after all the work she had done to have the glass and iron pergola at the corner of Frederick Douglass Avenue and Twelfth Street restored.

In the 1800s like most cities, the main form of transportation in Harbor City was the streetcar. Some were pulled by horses, but many were by then electrified. The last trolley ran in 1938, thanks to the efforts of the automobile industry. That was due to the simple fact that trolley lines could not keep up with the creation of roads and the desire of workers to travel on their own to work.

The glass and iron pergola was a triangular structure. The Victorian-style, triangular structure was long and high and supported by a series of iron columns. Plenty of room for people to stay dry and not rub elbows. It featured ornate iron decorations, a glass roof, an underground public bathroom featuring terrazzo floors, brass and nickel fixtures, and white Alaskan marble stalls. The rail service ended in 1938, and the bathroom was closed, never to be opened again. The ornate iron work was once the pride of Harbor City, but with the end of the trolly line and the repeated failures of the bus service, it fell into disrepair until Eve and other church ladies began to clamor for its restoration. When a delivery truck damaged it, there was talk of scrapping it, but there were suddenly insurance funds available and public interest, thanks to Eve and others, for it to be restored. After reviewing the original drawings, Eve and others realized that there had been two arch edicts made by the builders who designed the pergola, one of which was Black. The local Black Panther chapter criticized the use of public funds on an outdated, historic, little-used piece of iron and glass when the money could be used to support a preschool. They threatened that if it were restored, they would soon turn it into scrap iron and use the metal for bullets. Such was what they had implied to a local journalist.

Eve and a couple of others took pies and cakes with them to talk to the young bucks who listened with scowls and glares like Huey Lewis and Eldridge Cleaver displayed in Oakland. Eve came home in tears because they had spent so much time and energy to give the community something to be proud of, and all the young ones wanted to do was tear it down. Silas had listened. That night he came to the Black Panther chapter with over fifty members of the Buffalo Soldiers and thirty-five members of the local chapter of the Center Point Snake Eye Motorcycle Club. Each rider had a .45 strapped to his hip and a baseball bat strapped to his motorcycle. They revved their engines until the Black Panthers stepped outside with guns, clubs, and attitude. The message was simple. They could be united in civic pride and make certain that the pergola was never vandalized or damaged, or they would soon learn that the oppression of the political system and police was the least of their problems. As a sign of their sincerity, a couple of the bikers prepared Molotov cocktails while the speakers expounded. From time to time, the buildings near the pergola were tagged with gang signs, but it never was vandalized.

The pergola was three blocks from his home. On the plaque rededicating it after it was restored were the names of both architects and the owners of the foundry that had restored the pergola. He walked more slowly than he usually did. But he found if he kept his pace and held his head high, his headache did not return. Still, there was a strong throb at the base of his head.

He needed to sit down, but all of the benches were taken. A man named Riley was sitting on one of the benches. He was a white guy in his fifties with dirty hair and yellow teeth. He claimed that he was rich, but whenever Silas saw him he was always begging for money and claiming he was broke. Once Silas had given him ten dollars and then saw him stuff the ten into a wallet filled with twenties. He was a liar. He always claimed that he couldn't hear you, but if you offered him five bucks, he could suddenly hear. Bending over, Riley pressed a finger against the side of his nose and blew out some snot.

"Show a little respect!" shouted Silas.

"What?" barked Riley as he blew more snot out of the other side of his nose.

"Stop!" yelled Silas, holding out a five-dollar bill.

"What do you want?" asked Riley as he hacked up yellow phlegm.

"Move away," snapped Silas, grabbing at Riley's coat. "I need to sit down. You need to leave."

Without warning, Riley leaped to his feet and shoved Silas against an iron pillar. Silas crumpled to the ground and laid there motionless and silent.

5

Routines define the man, but what is it that drives the man into the routines whether he loves them or not? Like his father, John Abel never needed an alarm clock and always woke up early. It was just five o'clock, and he was wide awake trying to hang onto his dream. Like a mischievous spirit, it had taunted him since he was a child. He found it hard to listen to his father cough and spit while sitting on the toilet smoking two Chesterfields before he shaved. Then he went away to return in the evening for supper, only to disappear again. He seemed to always have a meeting to go to – either to the Elks, American Legion or VFW – all of which he was a member. The dream came later after he learned about the day his mother had collapsed on their kitchen floor with a cerebral hematoma. She was feeding him at the time it happened, and he was told there was cereal and milk all over the floor, and he was screaming. Did he remember it, or had someone implanted a memory into the reptilian part of his brain where no verbal thought dared to go? He was only twenty-one months old when she died. An expert said that age was too young for him to have a memory or recollection of the event. But what did those experts really know? It's not like they were experts when they were twenty-one months old. The ability to reach into your own, let alone another's memory, is not measurable by scales and test tubes.

When he was younger, he had dreams of being a drunken wandering poet like Li Po who could write a hundred verses per gallon of wine. But while he drank like he imagined Li Po did, he didn't have the talent nor a desire to be poor. After a few nose bumps and paws in his face by his golden retriever, Barney, Abel finally got up. He made

42

coffee, fed the cats, Alfie and Tessa, and the dogs, Barney and Murphy, brought in the newspaper, swallowed several vitamins and then poured his coffee. Then he returned to bed to read the paper, poems and meditation books on his iPad and waited for his wife, Billie, to wake up. It was a routine far from the solitary routine of his father, but he was as true to it as his father was to his.

On Friday mornings, the routine was different. Each Friday morning after his father had shaved and slapped Old Spice After Shave on his face, they would go to the Grill Café for breakfast. Each Friday Abel would have three pancakes, three link sausages, and orange juice. His father only drank black coffee. In the summer months the patrons would joke with him about how far out the Cubs were from first place. His father was from the north side of Chicago and had lived only a block from Wrigley Field. One year before the All Star Game, it was impossible for them to win the pennant because they were so far down in the cellar. He asked his father one time why he didn't root for a team that won games, and his father simply said that anyone can root for a winner.

While Abel was reading the comics, Billie rose and got herself a cup of coffee. He gave her the front section and opened up his iPad. That was when he realized that it was his father's birthday. He had known it was coming up soon, but he'd lost track of the days. If his father were still alive, he would have been one hundred and eleven years old. But, he had been dead for over fifty years. Every day he thought about his father, but that morning was filled with more than the usual nostalgia. He opened up the Pages program on his iPad and wrote down:

The Mathematics of Aging

When I was 22
My father died when he was 61
That was in 1971
It seemed that he died old.

Now in 2021
When I am 72
He seems to have died young.

His words were like
The wind. I thought
They would always
Come again.

I asked his advice about
Two girls I was torn between
He said anyone can
Learn to cook
Not everyone knows
How to party.

Now his words
Come every day
He is always older
And often wiser.

     He reread what he had written and then shared it
with Billie. "Nice," she said, and then added, "Aren't
poems supposed to rhyme?"
     "At the next vacancy for muse, don't bother
applying. You'd just crush some poor poet's soul."

"Let the games begin," She smiled and went back to her newspaper while Abel moved on to the BBC website.

"Have you heard from Riley lately?" Billie asked.

"Not for a while," said Abel. "He came by to bum some money from me a couple of weeks ago, and I didn't give him what he wanted."

"He may not be by for a while. He's charged with murder."

"Riley's more bark and bluster than anything else."

"He is charged with killing a man at a bus stop," said Billie, pointing to an article from one of the inside pages of the newspaper. "According to one witness, suddenly without provocation, Riley lunged at the man and tossed him against a metal post. Attempts to revive the man failed at the hospital."

"Riley?" Abel shook his head. "Where is he?"

"He's in jail, of course. Tell me you won't waste your time on him."

"I just asked where he was."

"You told me that he was banned from the Mission for fighting."

"They let him come and eat; they just won't let him stay the night. That's just the one here in Harbor City. He's not banned from all of the Missions."

"Hardly a ringing endorsement, counselor," smiled Billie. "The man is a con man, a mooch and never grateful. Why do you care about him? Prison may be the best thing for him. All he has been doing for years is living in squalor or on the streets. Why do you care what happens to him? You did your best for him."

"Who said I care?" asked Abel, who was already scanning the court files to find out who was Riley's attorney. It was an attorney he didn't know. Most likely a new attorney with little experience. The declaration of probable cause claimed that several witnesses had seen the assault, and all agreed that it was a senseless attack upon a man well known in the community for his faith and positive attitude.

"Wait, Wait, there's more," said Billie. "This is from the paper, 'The victim, Silas Smith, was a Navy Veteran, a widower, who was beloved and known to many in the community. He is best remembered for the colorful suits he wore, holding onto his Bible, and smiling. He talked to everyone who would speak with him about the Lord and any problems they might have.' This is what the paper says," Billie said. Peering over her readers like a school teacher, she added, "Your boy is so screwed."

"He is not my 'boy.' I haven't seen him for a while."

"There's more," beamed Billie. Reading again from the article, "'One witness said the victim was a cultural icon who gave his heart and soul to the community.'"

"I remember him from the mall, but I never talked to him," said Abel.

"He was the one with the yellow and red suits. Even purple. He wore hats that matched his suits," said Billie. "Want to make a bet that they have a statue in the park for him before your boy gets life?"

"I repeat, he is not my 'boy,' and I am not his lawyer," laughed Abel.

"Sweetie, this is your wife you are talking to. You can't help yourself."

After he showered and ate breakfast, Abel went to his backyard orchard with two large colanders. He filled one with ripe purple Italian plums. He filled the other one with Shiro plums, some of which were still slightly green. But he knew they would ripen on the shelf. He rinsed them off in cold water, dried them, and put them into two separate grocery bags.

He drove a couple of blocks to his church and found the minister in his study. The Episcopal Priest waved to him and thanked him for the fresh fruit. "The Food Bank never has enough fresh food. Do you have a moment?" Father Martin said, as he motioned toward a captain's chair on the other side of his desk. Father Martin's first name was Martin, and his last name was a Polish name with lots of vowels to stumble over, so everyone called him Martin or Father Martin. He did not stand on formality, but he liked to be the one in charge of meetings, and he expected his word to be the last word. He was only sixty-five and had recently announced his retirement. If he had asked, Abel would have reminded him that Walter Cronkite, who retired as news anchor when he turned sixty-five, considered that the biggest mistake of his life. Since his opinion on Martin's decision wasn't asked for, Abel didn't offer it. If over thirty years of sobriety had taught Abel anything, it was that his opinion was best kept to himself if he wasn't asked for it.

Martin was over six feet tall, had an athletic build, and a natural tousle of gray hair. Depending on how long it was since his last haircut, the hairs on the back of his head looked like small puffballs or gray gossamer flags that couldn't contain the sunlight. He often wore Pendleton shirts, hiking shoes, or Birkenstock sandals. He was a native of California, but he had blended well into the Northwest.

Abel sat down. He had been a regular church goer for the past five years, mainly because of the warm welcome Father Martin gave him at the first service he attended with Father Martin presiding.

Abel was raised Catholic but had drifted away from the faith of his childhood for many years. He had attended a Catholic funeral a few years earlier, and the priest made a point of telling the parishioners that Communion was only for Catholics who had gone to confession in the last two years. That was when he realized that pretending he was somehow still connected to the church was useless. He simply was not, and he was not sure how he'd turned his back on the faith he had grown up with. A few weeks later he attended the Episcopal church. He appreciated that the mass was similar to the one he had grown up with. Father Martin, with outstretched hands, announced that all were welcome to take communion, or they could just come forward and receive a blessing. "Know that all are welcome at this altar," Father Martin said. Abel knew then that he had found a church with a faith that worked for him.

"I liked your article for the *Tartan*," began Martin, "but I corrected a few minor grammatical errors. I hope you don't mind." The *Tartan* was the parish's monthly newsletter. As a Vestry member, Abel had been asked to contribute an article. Martin handed him the corrected draft.

Why I am an Episcopalian

A few years ago, I bought a plaque at the Pacific Northwest Shop in Proctor that reads "Bidden or Not Bidden, God is Present." I believed it when I bought it, and I believe it even more now. I am no theologian and do not pretend to be. My spiritual journey is more like a stroll down a well-worn path than a path in an adventure story, but it is my story and helps to explain how it was that I came to St. Andrews and became a Vestry member.

I was raised Roman Catholic, but this past January, I was received into the Episcopalian church. My mother died when I was an infant, and I never really embraced the

48

idea that God had my best interests at heart. In college, I referred to myself as agnostic. I could never say that there was not a God, but I was comfortable straddling the fence of "maybe." Atheism just seemed the other side of the blind faith of snake handling. Both are just too extreme for my Midwestern sensibilities of moderation. I was born and raised in Iowa.

Many years later, when I found myself on my knees praying to be relieved of an obsession, I felt that my prayer was answered by a God. This was why I bought that plaque. Some say they give their lives up to the care of a God of their understanding. I used to say I gave my life up to the care of a God I did not understand.

I asked to be received into the Episcopalian church to formalize my commitment to the church. Because I was already confirmed as Catholic, I could not be confirmed as Episcopalian. In being received into the Episcopalian church, I did not renounce my Catholic confirmation, as one must do when becoming a naturalized citizen. I am not certain what the spiritual implications of this are, nor do I care. Does it mean that, if I get as far as the Pearly Gates, I will be considered a dual national of Catholic and Episcopalian faiths? Possibly. Does it matter? Better seating perhaps. Some, if not most, religious mysteries should remain mysterious.

A few years ago, I was in my hometown in Iowa, and my sister suggested we attend mass together. Prior to communion, the priest was animated in his words and gestures that by the power granted to him, the wine was no longer wine but the blood of Christ. I certainly admired his certitude of faith but questioned his understanding of chemistry and passed on communion.

At a funeral, when it came time for communion, the priest made a point of stating that those who were not

Catholic could not go forward for communion or for a blessing. He went so far as to add that if a person was Catholic, but had not been to confession in the past two years, then they should also stay in their seats.

Not long after this funeral, I attended mass at St. Andrews. As usual, Father Martin began the sermon with an introduction about how some were drawn to the church for reasons unknown to us, and so on. I liked that even though I could not tell you why I had dropped in, but I sincerely enjoyed the service and the similarities to the Catholic mass.

When Father Martin said that all were welcome to receive standard communion, a gluten-free wafer, wine or juice, or just a blessing, I liked that a lot. At the end of the service, Father Martin enthusiastically welcomed me. Over the next few years, I sporadically returned to St. Andrews. One day, Father Martin mentioned to me that services were held every Sunday. This got me thinking, and I made it a New Year's resolution to attend weekly services, which I continue to do as best I can.

Even though I began attending on a regular basis, I still harbored questions about the level of my faith. One Sunday, while we were reading the Nicene Creed, I asked myself, "Why are you saying this out loud if you do not believe it?" In a flash, the answer came to me as simple as it was sudden. I do believe that Christ died, He was risen, and He will come again. I do believe in the Apostolic Church.

My early religious training was based on Baltimore Catechism in which for every mystery of faith, there is an answer.

The following are excerpts from the Wikipedia article on Transubstantiation:

The Roman Catholic Church teaches that in the Eucharistic offering, bread and wine are changed into the body and blood of Christ. The affirmation of this doctrine was expressed, using the word "transubstantiate," by the Fourth Council of the Lateran in 1215. It was later challenged by various 14th-century reformers, John Wycliffe in particular...

As with all Anglicans, Anglo-Catholics and other High Church Anglicans historically held belief in the real presence of Christ in the Eucharist but were "hostile to the doctrine of transubstantiation."

As often as I can, I come to the Wednesday noon service to take communion and to listen to the sermons that tend to be more informal, often focusing on the life of the Saint whose feast day it may be. It is a small group, even smaller than the 8 a.m. service. I truly enjoy being able to greet everyone with the peace of the Lord.

I enjoy knowing that I am in a church where priests can marry, where women can be priests, and where sexual orientation are not matters of sin. I do believe that "Bidden or Not Bidden, God is Present," but God seems just a tad closer when I take communion. The power of communion cannot be underestimated. I recommend the book, The Priest Barracks, by Guillaume Zeller. It is a powerful depiction of faith, the power of forgiveness, and the importance of communion.

Some spiritual experiences come as sudden as a flash of light, such as with Saul on the road to Damascus. Other spiritual experiences are gradual and are considered spiritual experiences of the educational variety. I think that whether or not we recognize it, everything we do is a spiritual experience – consider the simple act of pausing to help someone rather than moving past. Not all spiritual experiences must have a positive outcome; some experiences draw us closer to a loving God while others may be backward steps taking us away from a loving God; just like good diet and exercise, all of these experiences shape who we are.

I have no quarrel with my Catholic upbringing, any more than I dispute the majesty of the Cologne Cathedral, Dante's Comedy, or the beauty of the Sistine Chapel. I do not believe that these and many other works – for example, the work of Martin Luther and the writings of C.S. Lewis – could have been created by secular inspiration alone.

I have trust in a faith, such as ours, that allows for unresolved mysteries. I was raised in one faith, but believe I was born to be an Episcopalian. I searched for years without even knowing that I was on a quest, and now I have come home to a faith that works for me. I am very glad to be on the Vestry and grateful for the opportunities to serve, and in some small way, help others understand the power and grace of our faith.

Abel scanned the draft slowly. He had no idea what changes Martin made and really didn't care all that much. "Changes look good. Thanks for catching my mistakes."

"Glad to be of service. So what kind of lawyer are you?" asked Martin.

"Not bad. What kind of priest are you?"

"All purpose," smiled the priest.

"That is the kind of lawyer I am. Why do you ask?"

"There is a parishioner that comes to the 10 o'clock service that is in need of a lawyer. Her daughter gave away custody of her two sons and now regrets it. Roberta, which is her name, wants to know what she can do to help herself I asked some other lawyers in the parish, and they all recommended you."

"Custody once decided by a court is one of the hardest to undo."

"But could you talk to her? Even if you can't help her, maybe you can refer her to someone who can. You probably know someone who is perhaps a cut or two above just 'not bad.'" Smiled the priest.

"The plums are good. Make sure that some of them get to the Food Bank," Abel said as he got up with a laugh.

<u>6</u>

Abel's office was a two-story house built in 1900 as a boarding house and sometime in the 1980s converted into an office. The owner, before Abel and another lawyer bought the building, was an interior design business that had installed large desks suitable for rolling out blueprints. Abel had repainted the interior and had new carpet and tile laid down, but he'd not disturbed the built-in desks on the first floor. When the other lawyer moved out and declared bankruptcy, Abel was faced with the choice of selling his share or buying out the other lawyer's interest. He wanted the other lawyer gone anyway and had even offered to buy him out. But he didn't have any interest in packing up over thirty years of files and knick knacks. So he was more than happy to buy the other lawyer's interest in the building from the bankruptcy court at a better price than what he'd offered his former business partner. There was room for at least one more, if not three other lawyers, in the building, but Abel enjoyed his privacy and had no interest in renting out any of the rooms. His main office was on the second floor. However, when he was expecting someone, like now, he unlocked the front door and set up his laptop on a desk to greet his guest.

Exactly at the agreed upon time, David Levi Yabroff greeted Abel at the door with a smile and salutation less enthusiastic than he usually displayed. He was in his middle forties but completely bald. He had broad shoulders and a round face, and he obviously loved food. He was wearing a jacket with a canvas messenger bag slung over his shoulder and positioned in front of him. Abel could tell that within a concealed compartment was probably a stainless steel Ruger .357 Magnum revolver with a 2.25-inch barrel.

If Yabroff were not carrying the weapon when he was attacked in a YMCA parking lot, there was a good chance he would have suffered far more than a concussion. Abel had seen the surveillance video and was certain Yabroff's attacker had no desire to stop punching him until he pulled out his .357. Abel thought it was a clear case of self-defense and showed great restraint under pressure. Yabroff pointed the gun and watched the man retreat to the other side of the parking lot and begin insulting him. The original prosecutor who charged the case saw things differently than Abel and charged Yabroff with felony assault. But once the case was assigned to an experienced prosecutor, Abel secured an agreed dismissal. It had taken time, though, because Yabroff was a seaman whose schedule was two months on land and four months at sea. He was originally offered a misdemeanor and a suspended sentence with dismissal of the case if he maintained law abiding behavior. However, Yabroff turned down the offer each time because he was innocent. Nothing gums up the legal system like an innocent man demanding justice. Guilty guys take deals; even innocents take deals to avoid risks, but not Yabroff. He wanted his day in court. Eventually the prosecutor simply decided that it wasn't worth the trouble to possibly convict an innocent man in the name of justice.

Yabroff's first name was David, but everyone who knew him called him Levi. He once said that whenever he received a call and the first word was David, he knew it was a sales pitch. Yabroff collapsed and sat in the chair opposite Abel as he let out a long sigh, finishing with a yawn. Abel enjoyed Levi's company because he had an active mind and was talented in many ways. He was a master electrician and locksmith. At one time, when they were eating at a Chinese restaurant, he knew by smell alone that the tea was a blend of jasmine and oolong tea leaves.

"That is a long sigh."

"I've had a long couple of days," replied Levi. "My trailer was broken into, and a lot of my stuff was trashed."

"That's too bad," said Abel. "Was anything taken?"

"No, it was just broken into and trashed. A few things broken, and family stuff strewn around."

The trailer was more of an outpost than a home. Levi had a wife and a daughter in the Philippines. The trailer was mainly a place where he slept between his travels at sea or to his home.

"That's not all. My van was broken in as well."

"Was it next to the trailer?"

"No, I store it on a lot while I'm at sea or in the Philippines. It is not far from the trailer park, though. Someone took a knife to the seats and a few tools were scattered around but again, nothing was taken."

"Sounds like someone was after you."

Levi nodded with a grim expression. "My storage unit was broken into as well. I am not sure when that happened, but the security footage is of no help. My storage unit is in a building where only the entrance and exit are videotaped. No camera is on the door to the unit."

"You think it was all one person?"

"I am certain of it, and I'm certain it was Benis Dalton. His wife is a Deputy Sheriff and he's a realtor. Between them they must have figured out where my trailer is located, my van is stored, and where I keep my things when I'm at sea."

"Perhaps they learned where everything else was when they broke into your trailer."

Levi shrugged. "Possible," he conceded, "but it was Dalton. I am sure of that."

"I don't disagree with you. I just don't know how we could prove it. Have you ever heard of Locard's Exchange Principle? Locard was known as the French Sherlock Holmes, but he was the real deal. He was a pioneer in forensic evidence. He believed that every criminal leaves behind trace evidence. It's because of him that you see technicians scouring and searching every inch of a crime scene today. Like most general principles, however, it has flaws. There are many reasons why evidence may be lost, destroyed, or the evidence collected is misleading."

"Maybe so, but I've cleaned up, and I doubt that the police would invest much time investigating a property crime."

"Major crimes get major workups and minor crimes such as vandalism do not. Still, you should file a police report. Even if they do nothing but log in an incident report, it might help you with an insurance claim."

"Seems like a waste of time, but I will do that. I'm sick of this state, and I think that I will move to Florida."

"Can you sail out of Florida?"

"In time I could probably find a ship. If not, I can fly in and out of this state to get on a ship. I started the visa process, so my wife and daughter can join me. I'd rather she grow up in Florida than here where there are so many liberals in power with too many notions about what is right and wrong. I doubt a Florida prosecutor would have even charged me."

"I can't disagree," Abel said. He might have said more, but he was interrupted by a loud knock on the front door. Then the door swung open, and a man entered with the obvious intention of interrupting whatever was going on in the office. He was in his forties with a severe sunburn and deep lines on his face. He was wearing blue jeans and a denim shirt. He wore a backpack and a fanny pack in front.

"I'm here for Sean Riley," he announced.

"He is not here," replied Abel.

"I know he's not here. He is in jail."

"Why did you ask for him?" asked Abel, rising up from his seat.

"I wasn't asking for him. I'm here on his behalf," stammered the man. "He wants to see you," he said to Abel. "He's tried to call you, but you have not answered his calls."

Abel shook his head and said, "I have not had any phone calls from him."

"He's tried to call you, but he's in jail, and his phone calls are blocked. Do you know who I am?"

"I forget your name. I remember you from the homeless encampment near the river. You had a Remington 552 BDL Speedmaster." Looking at Levi, he added, " Beautiful walnut stock with a brass deflector."

"My name is Rob Washington."

"Are you still out at the encampment by the river?"

"No, Gus Huffman, the State Game Enforcement Officer, finally got us shut down and persuaded my ex-wife to file another complaint against me. This time she said that she feared for her life if I had a gun. My rifle is now in storage with the Sheriff's Office. I think he is long-dicking my wife now, but I can't prove it. I can't even get within one thousand feet of her or see my kids until I get evaluated for domestic violence. If I say that I didn't do anything, they say I'm a liar. You're a lawyer, and you know how a lawyer's lies work."

"I don't know what I can do for Riley."

"You can defend him. That's what you can do. He's innocent!" shouted Washington.

"I don't think Riley would ever try to hurt anyone."

"I was there. All he did was stand up, and the man fell backwards."

"How do you know that?"

"I was there."

"Did you tell the police what happened?"

"No."

"Why not?"

"This is why not," Washington said, pulling a revolver from his fanny pack. It was a stainless steel gun.

Washington waved the gun in the air and pointed it at Abel. "This is why. If I talked to the police, they would have run a check on me and found there is a restraining order out on me. I'm not supposed to have a gun, and I had this on me." He jabbed and jerked the gun as if making punctuation marks in the air.

Levi shifted around and slipped his right hand into a compartment in his backpack. With his hand, Abel motioned for Levi to do nothing.

"Put the gun away and tell me what happened," Abel said.

"Do guns make you nervous?"

"Only the ones pointed at me. Put it away if you want me to listen to you."

Washington put the gun back in his fanny pack, but didn't zip it up. "We were at the bus stop waiting for a bus to take us out to the motel where we're staying. Riley has a room there, and he was letting me crash in his room. I stepped away to get us a couple of subway sandwiches. There is a Subway shop only a half block from the bus stop. I was coming back and only a few feet away when Riley stood up, and the man fell backwards. He didn't hit

59

the man. Anyway, a crowd started gathering and yelling at Riley. Then two police cars pulled over and backed the crowd away. Everyone was yelling about how Riley had attacked the man, but I had the gun and didn't want to say anything. There might be a warrant out for my arrest."

"A warrant for what?"

"What does it matter? There might not be one. At most, it's just a misunderstanding with a shop owner that I can clear up."

"So you left and let Riley be arrested without saying anything?"

"Yeah, what else could I do? But I'm here now trying to make it right. I know he wants you to see him."

"How do you know that?"

"He's in a jail pod with a friend of mine. My friend called and told me that Riley wants to see you. He told me that Riley thinks of you as an uncle."

"You have noticed that he's delusional from time to time, haven't you?"

"Just talk to him," begged Washington as he backed out the door.

7

On Wednesdays at noon, Abel often went to the Eucharist service. It was not a well-attended service. Only seven or so regularly attended. When Abel saw an elderly woman sitting next to a younger woman, he assumed they were Roberta and Denise Jarad. Father Martin had not only told Abel about them, he'd gone so far as to set up a meeting after the service. Abel nodded in their direction, and the older woman nodded back at him. She was small in frame but sat up very straight, making all the few inches of her frame count. The older woman had short gray hair and a pale complexion. The younger woman was heavyset with rounded features and full lips. From her features and complexion, Abel deduced that she had Indian and Pacific Islander blood in her veins. She shyly smiled at Abel which was more noncommittal than welcoming.

The noon service was always shorter than the Sunday service. The Nicene Creed was not said, as it was reserved for Sundays and major feasts. Abel had no idea why. Perhaps it was a concession for those who attended while on their lunch hour. Neither the Nicene Creed nor shorter Apostles' Creed contained a prayer for the conversion of the Jews.As they had when Abel was a child. Whether this was a concession on the limits of prayer or somehow considered more politically correct, he did not know.

At Sunday service Martin spoke from the pulpit and intertwined his personal thoughts with the required readings from the Old Testament and the New Testament. In a three-year cycle, all of the Bible was read to the congregation, except perhaps for some passages in Leviticus and Deuteronomy. Occasionally, his remarks dealt more with the barbecue and the price of animals than the interior design of the temple.

On Wednesdays, Father Martin stood in the middle between the left and right altar rails and delivered a homily usually based on a saint whose feast day had either recently passed or was soon to be celebrated before the next Sunday. In general, he talked about whoever he wanted. One time he talked about Frederick Douglass simply because he was a person whose life he thought we should never forget. Abel preferred the low keyed informality over lectures from the pulpit.

"Today, I would like to talk about Saint Nicholas," began Father Martin. "His feast day is not this week, but there isn't another saint who really interests me today. So I want to talk about Saint Nicholas of Myra, also known as Nicholas of Bari. He's known as Saint Nicholas for the many miracles ascribed to his intercession. He was the patron saint of sailors, merchants, archers, repentant thieves, prostitutes, children, brewers, pawnbrokers, unmarried people, and students in various cities and countries around Europe. He apparently has a broad appeal to many different people," smiled Martin. "While not much is known about his life, we know his habit of secret gift giving gave rise to the traditional model of Santa Claus.

Very little is known about his life, but an early list makes him an attendee at the First Council of Nicaea in 325, but he is never mentioned in any writings by people who were actually at the Council. I don't know why. Some say he was defrocked or in prison for slapping the heretic Arius at the Council sessions, but I do not know why it is not mentioned by the contemporary writers at the Council.

One legend has it that he resurrected three children who were pickled in brine and going to be sold as ham by a butcher during a famine."

Martin shrugged his shoulders and continued on. "Another story that comes down to us is that he was born into a wealthy family. When he learned that three daughters were in danger of becoming prostitutes because they had no dowery, he secretly passed sacks of gold through a window so their father would have money to give as a dowery. I suppose this is part of the basis for his connection to Santa Claus.

Another story says that he saved three innocent men from execution. Fewer than 200 years after Nicholas' death, the St. Nicholas Church was built in Myra under the orders of Theodosius II. Even though some of the legends and stories ascribed to him are far-fetched, there is no doubt that he was a real person who lived a pious and generous life. His acts of quiet kindness touched many lives, both in his lifetime and now in ours. Each year his acts of kindness are celebrated worldwide by people who may not even know that he existed. Such is the power of unseen generosity. I commend him to you," finished Father Martin.

After the service, Father Martin, Roberta and Denise Jarad, and Abel gathered in Father Martin's office around a large conference table. Martin sat on one end, Roberta and Denise sat together on one side, and Abel sat at the other end of the table.

"As you might have surmised, I am not Denise's biological mother," said Roberta. "My late husband and I adopted her from an orphanage out of India when she was three." She continued, "We adopted another girl from the same orphanage who is doing fine. Regrettably, Denise has always had problems, but I love them both just the same."

"That's good to hear," said Abel. He wondered how often Denise had heard that she was loved the same as her sister despite her problems.

"She is a little slow and trusting of others she should not trust," continued Roberta. "I just don't know why you didn't come to me if you needed help."

"Mom, you told me to take care of the kids and learn to take care of myself. That is what I thought I was doing."

"Well, you were fooled by a supreme con artist, if you ask me."

"Perhaps Denise could tell me what happened," said Father Martin.

"I can tell you what happened. She was hoodwinked into giving up her children," snapped Roberta. With a huff she crossed her arms across her chest. "And now I have to bail her and the kids out."

"Nevertheless, I'd like to hear from Denise what happened."

"Where should I start?"

"Somewhere near the beginning is usually best," suggested Abel. "I know a little about the problem from Father Martin. You have two boys who you gave up custody to, and now you want the boys back. But what led to you giving them away?"

"Linda Garvey promised me that it would be temporary. She told me that she would teach me to take care of the boys, and when I was ready, I could have them back."

"I think we are far from the beginning, but why couldn't she teach you to parent without taking custody of them?"

"She said that she needed to have custody so she could get a large house for all of us. She needed to have custody to qualify for aid."

"Why didn't you ask for aid on your own?" demanded Roberta.

"I don't know. It was all so complicated," shrugged Denise. "I was Linda's caregiver . I had the job through the Korean Women's Association. Sometimes the boys would join me when I went to her apartment to clean. She was always friendly and saw that I had trouble controlling them. This was even before their father committed suicide."

"The father committed suicide?" asked Abel.

"My oldest boy, Randy, found him when he was six. We were at the park playing and Randal, my husband, had parked on the other side of the park. We saw him pull up, but he didn't get out of the car. We waited for him, but when he didn't come over, Randy ran to the car and found his father with a gunshot to his head. He'd put a gun into his mouth."

"Why?"

Denise shook her head and finally said, "He was a custodian at a junior high school. Some students said he touched them inappropriately, and he'd just lost his job. He was escorted from the school, then he drove to the park and shot himself. Randy was carrying a child's baseball bat that his father gave him. They'd gotten it at a minor league game. Randy treasured it. He was knocking on the window trying to wake his dad up. I will never forget that."

"The father always seemed a little odd to me," interjected Roberta.

"After he killed himself, I started receiving money for each of the boys from Social Security. It's survivor's benefits and intended for their welfare. Once Linda learned that I was getting money, she began to pester me about moving in with her. Then she said that she should be their custodian. I agreed, but she never let me move in."

"Now we can't even see the boys," added Roberta. "I've called her myself, and she just says the boys are busy. Every time I've called, she tells me that they have plans."

65

"After she got custody, she contacted Social Security and asked that their benefits be sent to her. Because she's their custodian, the Public Housing Authority made arrangements for her to have a bigger house. Whenever I ask about moving in with her and the boys, she just says 'not yet.' She says I'm not ready to be their full-time mother."

"Can you help them?" asked Father Martin.

Abel shrugged and asked, "Were you in court when she got custody?'

"I didn't know about it until after she got custody," replied Roberta.

"But, Denise, were you there?"

"Yes."

"Did the judge or commissioner ask why you were giving up custody of your children to a single woman?" He paused and asked, "She's not married, is she?"

"No, she's not married. She told the judge that she was going to teach me how to be a good parent. She said that was why she was taking custody. To protect the boys and help me. Does that make a difference?"

"It may. All third-party custody arrangements are subject to modification. Before you ask, a third-party modification is a custody case in which custody was granted to someone other than a parent."

"You could have asked me," wailed Roberta.

"Mom, you told me to take care of things on my own. That is what I was doing."

"Who knew you would make such a hash of it?"

"Can you help them?" repeated Father Martin.

"We need to do two things. First, Roberta should file a petition for custody on her own. Second, Denise should file a petition in the custody case requesting that the custody order be modified. There is a possibility that the petition to modify might be tossed out if the court finds that there isn't adequate cause to go forward. Adequate cause means a change in circumstances. The change would be Garvey's desire to welch on the deal of giving you back custody. Roberta's petition would be a safety net in the event that a court finds that Denise is not a fit parent and Garvey is not a suitable custodian. If that happened, then Roberta could be named custodian."

"How much will this cost?" Roberta asked.

"I'm not cheap. I appreciate the story of Saint Nicholas giving away money, but he came from a rich family. However, I don't, and I need to be paid for the work I do."

"You know about Nicholas?" asked Martin.

"I read things. I know that Arius is considered a heretic because he did not believe that Christ existed until he was born of the Virgin Mary. At the Council, it was determined that Christ, like God, had always been. Personally I think he might have had a point. God is always God in the Old Testament. Christ is never mentioned as the Son in waiting. For that matter, neither is the Holy Ghost. Some mysteries are better left unexplored, I suppose. Thoughts that used to get a man burned at the stake can now be made into best sellers."

"How much will it cost?" Roberta asked again.

"The short answer is, I do not know. But from what you've told me, Garvey will fight to keep the money rolling in from the kids."

"You do not know how vicious she is," warned Denise.

"If you come to the office in the morning, we can talk about my retainer. I want to look at the court file before the three of us sign any contracts."

"Why can't we talk about the contracts now?" demanded Roberta.

"I want to look at the file. Besides, I prefer not to do business in a church. Christ tossed the money lenders and sellers of doves out of the temple. Haven't you also noticed that the priest always wants a cut of the action? Isn't that what tithing is, Father?"

"I will keep you in my prayers, my son," smiled Father Martin. "I fear that you know all too well what you do."

"Both Denise and Roberta will have to sign agreements that I can represent them. Then if they come into disagreement, I will have to withdraw and cannot represent either of them."

"Why is that? I am the one paying your fee."

"Because you are both my clients. Where the money comes from does not determine who my client is."

"There will not be any disagreement between us. We both want the boys away from that woman."

"That is true," said Denise.

"There is one more thing," said Abel. "I do not want to ever hear again that where we are is Denise's fault."

"But…" started Roberta.

"I don't care what you think. I actually like the Zen saying that a person should never complain about anything, not even to himself. But I know that is impossible. I have often tried it between terrible golf swings and other things. But I am serious about this. I do not care what you think about whose fault it is, or what you may say to Denise when I am not around. But if you say it is her fault, then I am out of both cases. So think about that. If you cannot agree to do that, then I don't want either of you as a client. You can tell me what you decide in the morning. You do not have to hire me."

As Roberta's head pivoted toward Denise, her slight smile slipped away into a solemn straight line.

8

The isolation cell where Sean Riley was housed was in the
Three South Unit of the Hardin County Department of
Corrections. Three South was where juveniles charged as
adults, mental cases, disciplinary problems, and those who
needed to be kept out of the general population for their
safety, such as lawyers and police officers, were housed.
Abel passed through the first gate of the sally port and told
the guard that he wanted to speak with Riley. The guard
pointed to one of the rooms between the two gates and said,
"He's already in there with two others. You will have to
stand. I already told the one lawyer that the limit was two
chairs. It's a safety issue."

"That's fine," said Abel.

"Once inside, you will be locked inside."

"That's new," said Abel.

The guard sighed, "Yes, it's a new safety
precaution. There is a button to push when you want to
leave or if a fight breaks out."

"Locking lawyers inside with deranged clients is
best for unit safety."

The guard shook his head and smiled, "I don't make
the rules, Mr. Abel. I just enforce them."

Riley was seated on the far side of the narrow table
facing the door as required by the jailhouse protocol.
Incarceration seemed to suit him well. He was far cleaner
than when Abel had last seen him, and while still thin, he
wasn't gaunt. His wrists were cuffed and attached to a waist
restraint. When he saw Abel, he grunted and smiled which
Abel took as about as warm of a greeting as the man
usually gave him.

Seated across from Riley was his guardian, Raven Oakes. Oakes and Abel had disliked one another for years. She considered him an arrogant lawyer who knew a little about a lot of things, but thought of himself as an expert in all things. She was a few years younger than Abel but had been a lawyer longer. Abel hadn't become a lawyer until his middle thirties. She owned a guardianship agency and was the legal counsel for the agency. Her year-end accounts to the courts revealed that her services were often used. Over the years, she had taken on more weight until her chin disappeared into her neck, giving her a resemblance to a toad or frog. Considering her ability to snap up fees and excessive costs from clients by using her verbal skills with the speed of a frog or toad snagging flies made the analogy seem most appropriate.

Standing next to Oakes was a young public defender, Michael Rosekrans, who Abel had occasionally encountered in the felony courts. He was thin like a long distance runner and had jet black hair. When Abel entered the room, Rosekrans extended his hand and thanked him for coming.

"You invited him?" snapped Oakes.

"Riley said he would not take the deal until he spoke to Abel."

"But you are his lawyer," pressed Oakes.

"That I am, but he said that he wanted to talk to Abel, and as his lawyer, I have an obligation to respect a client's request."

"So what is the offer?"

"They are offering the low end of the sentencing range for second-degree murder, fifteen years."

"You couldn't get the offer down to manslaughter with an offer under ten years?"

"Eunnie Hong is the prosecutor. You know how she is. She won't budge below second-degree murder. The witnesses, and there are many, all say that he attacked the victim without provocation. The victim is a well-known figure in the community. You may have seen him at the mall. He was the guy in colorful suits who walked around the mall with a Bible in his hand. Eunnie says that manslaughter is not possible, and if we go to trial, she will also enter a finding that this is a hate crime and request a sentence outside the standard range."

"Eunnie does like to turn the screws when she can," Abel agreed.

"He should take the offer, and you should tell him to take the offer," said Oakes. Then she added. "It's a good offer. I've read the file, and he needs to be off the street. Prison might save his life. He needs structure. He looks better now than I've seen him in years."

"He does look fed," said Abel. "While he's in prison will you still be collecting your monthly fee from the VA as his payee?"

"That has nothing to do with it. He is guilty and needs to avoid as much prison time as possible. Given his mental history, I wouldn't be surprised if he doesn't end up in a nice minimum security unit with an understanding staff."

"The way you say that, it almost sounds like Club Med. Do you expect daily saunas and weekly massages where he might end up?"

"No one is saying that. I have not told him that prison was a good deal. But I did tell him that there is a good chance of conviction if we go to trial. I am not trying to force him into taking the deal. I just think it's the best thing to do," interjected Rosekrans. "I have gotten the best offer I'm going to get from Eunnie. If he doesn't take the offer, we'll go to trial."

"Look at him," demanded Oakes. "Imagine how he will do in front of a jury." she added, pointing at Riley. He stuck his tongue out at her in response.

"Have you spoken to Rob Washington?" asked Abel.

"Who's that?" asked Rosekrans.

"He's Riley's friend and a freeloader. He was staying in Riley's motel room until we kicked him out," said Oakes.

"You kicked him out?" Asked Abel.

"That is the rule at the motel where Riley was staying. Washington was crashing there, and that's not allowed. So he got kicked out, and Riley stormed off with him."

"What did you mean you kicked him out? Do you own the motel?" Able demanded

"I am part owner. I am a partner in the LLC that now owns the motel."

"Who else is in the LLC?"

"None of your business."

"I can get the information online from the Secretary of State."

"The LLC is F&O. My partner is Carl Friendly."

"Officer Friendly?" Asked Abel.

"Yes."

"Last time I spoke with him, he was busy enforcing the drug busts at the motel. Did he finally drive the owners into selling for a song? Lucky you to be in business with him.

"I resent your implication. The owners could not keep the place drug-free, and the bank would not renew their mortgage loan when it came due. It was up for sale, and we bought it. That's all there is to it."

"That's not all. You're his guardian who kicked him out onto the street. You are a guardian who made a ward homeless."

"He could have stayed without Washington, and I didn't kick him out. He broke the rules. He had an unregistered guest in his room, and the manager kicked him out. I didn't kick him out."

"Rent too high," barked Riley.

"It is a fair price!" yelled Oakes. "Plus, you drink and have torn out more than one microwave oven."

"How did he know you owned the motel?"

"I am just a partner in the partnership that owns the motel."

"How did he know that you owned a stake in it?"

"His friend Washington told him. Just like you, he knows how to get onto the Internet. Amazing the things a homeless man in a library can do rather than look for a job."

"Amazing. You're his guardian. When he was kicked out on the street, did you find him another place?"

"Look at him! No one wants him!" Oakes shouted. "This is about him not taking the prosecutor's offer."

"Have you talked to Washington?" Abel asked Rosekrans.

"I don't know who he is."

"He says that he saw the incident. He says Riley didn't touch Silas."

"They are friends. What do you expect him to say? I doubt he was even there," huffed Oakes.

"He saw!" barked Riley. "Washington rabbit hunter, he saw!"

74

"He's told you more than he's told me," said Rosekrans. "What do you want me to do?"

"Can I see the autopsy report?"

"Sure." Rosekrans took the report out of his briefcase and handed it to Abel who quickly scanned it.

"Did you talk to Dr. Steiner about his findings?"

Rosekrans shook his head. "No, I just read the report. It didn't seem necessary to set up an interview. Eunnie would just complain about it being a waste of time and most likely would withdraw her offer."

"I suppose, she might. Bad deals are like flies they come back no matter how you much you swat them away." said Abel. "I would like to talk to Riley alone now."

"He needs to take the offer, or it will be withdrawn," said Oakes.

"I doubt that," said Abel. He pushed the call button for the two lawyers to be let out of the room.

Abel sat down in front of Riley and placed a photograph of the pergola between them. "I took this yesterday. Can you tell me where you were, where the man who died was, and what happened?"

"I can't hear you!" barked Riley.

Abel pulled out a watermelon Jolly Rancher from his shirt pocket and held it up. "You can't smoke in here, and I can't give you money. But I can give you this to suck on and eat while we're here. You can't take it into your unit. The guards check for contraband. If I give this to you, will you be able to hear me?"

Riley nodded that he could, so Abel unwrapped it and gave it to Riley.

"You like me."

"Let's not push it," said Abel. "Tell me where you were."

With gestures and short responses, Riley explained that he was near the center of the pergola when Silas started yelling at him for no reason. He jumped up, and the man fell backwards.

"I thought he was drunk like me," whispered Riley. "He stumbled back. I tried to catch him, but he fell down in front of me."

"You didn't push him, or chest bump him?"

"No, no," said Riley. "He got in my face; I stood up; and he then fell back."

"People say you pushed him."

"People lie."

"Were you drunk?"

Riley wrinkled up his nose in thought. "Not very," he finally said.

"Maybe you pushed him and didn't know it."

"I did not touch him. Everyone who says that I pushed him are liars. I did not push him. Anyone who says I did is a liar."

"Why would they lie?"

Riley shook his head and bit his lip. "You are my friend. Will you help me?"

"Yes," said Abel.

Crunching down on the Jolly Rancher, Riley asked for another. Abel gave him a cherry one. They sat in silence until it was gone, and then Abel left.

9

McBride had just called the downstairs noon meeting of the
AA Fellowship to order when Abel walked in the door.
They shook hands as they always did, and Abel went
upstairs to a smaller meeting room. When McBride came to
his first meeting, Abel greeted him with a handshake, then
at the end of the meeting he again shook his hand and
encouraged him to come back. At first McBride thought it
odd that a white guy would welcome him back. He
suspected that Abel might be gay, but over time realized
that Abel had seen him in various courtrooms and merely
wanted him to stay sober.

The upstairs room was small with a small table. The
usual chairperson, Matt, was chatting with another regular,
George, who had over forty years of sobriety. Matt was a
retired boilermaker who was dyslexic. He often said that he
learned to read when he came into AA. With just the three
of them, there was over one hundred and ten years of
sobriety, and there were also others in the room.

"Abel's here. We should have a meeting," chuckled
George, shaking Abel's hand. Matt passed out sheets to
read, and as usual, he read the preamble, "What it is." After
the readings and introductions, Matt asked a retired
minister to read from the chapter *Women Suffer Too*. It was
Matt's favorite story. She was an early AA member. Abel
liked her story, but not as much as Matt. Whenever he was
asked to chair a meeting, he usually selected the passages
on the Third Step. The issue of turning one's will over to
the care of God never seemed like a done deal, no matter
how long a person had been sober. There were a couple of
new people in the group. Because it was a small group,
everyone got a chance to speak, and the topic quickly

evolved into the First Step because of the new people attending.

Abel usually kept his remarks short and more or less on topic. He took to heart when a friend of his often said that yesterday's sobriety won't keep you sober. So, he thought it important to talk about how he was feeling on the day of the meeting. He liked to follow the advice of the Greek Stoic Epictetus who is quoted as saying, "A man ought to know that it is not easy to have an opinion a fixed principle if he does not daily say the same things and hear the same things and apply them to his life." That was just one of the reasons why Abel kept his life close to AA.

When Abel was almost done speaking, he quoted from the end of *Freedom From Bondage*. "This great experience that released me from the bondage of hatred and replaced it with love is really just another affirmation of the truth I know. I get everything I need in Alcoholics Anonymous – everything I need I get – and when I get what I need, I invariably find that it was *just what I wanted all the time.*" Abel did not mean that everything he valued or treasured existed in AA. He simply meant that without AA and sobriety, he would not have the things he treasured, such as a life with Billie. He ended his five-minute speech by saying to the new guys, "Keep coming back and when you leave here, know where your next meeting will be."

George never knew a topic that didn't involve a trip down memory lane to when he was a street wino living in Portland Oregon. His first two sponsors were World War II Marine veterans. One had been a POW of the Japanese. George had sought him out believing that he hated the Japanese, and he could teach him to heal and stay sober. The veteran told him that he didn't hate the Japanese, and if George wanted to keep on hating, he might as well just go out and get drunk.

No matter how the meeting went or who spoke, Abel always walked away feeling better than when he had gone in. He had a simple belief that no one should leave a meeting without knowing where their next meeting was going to be. During his first meeting in AA, people hadn't talked about many things that went over his head, but all of them talked about staying sober one day at a time. So, he told a man, that he would be back the following noon because everyone had talked about it being a was a twenty-four-hour program, that all he had to do was stay sober twenty-four hours at a time. The man looked him the eye and said he could come back sooner, say to the six o'clock meeting. That simple advice had done more to keep Abel sober than all the spiritual things that were said. Just as George often told his story of recovery from hopelessness, Abel told that part of his story whenever there was a new person in the group.

After the upstairs group broke up, Abel found McBride for his usual handshake and to ask him for a favor. He pulled McBride aside and asked if he knew Linda Garvey.

"Who is she?" asked McBride.

Abel gave him a quick summary of the case and finished by saying, "I have a lot of declarations about what a wonderful person the grandmother is and how much she loves her grandchildren. The problem is that I don't have any information about Linda Garvey. Without that, the court might simply say that I have not shown why the children should not stay where they are."

"So you think because I'm Black and live in Center Point that I must know who she is?"

"You know a lot of people," stumbled Abel. "I think that you might know most everything that goes on in

Center Point. You know a lot of criminals too. As I recall, many of them are your cousins and nephews."

"I'm just giving you a hard time," smiled McBride. "She's not any blood relative of mine, but I can ask around. I appreciate what you do."

"I appreciate what you do too," said Abel. "You not only had the idea of providing meals to the children of Center Point, but you put it into action."

"Speaking of that, I may need some help from you. Molly Chrysler gave me some money to feed the children in Center Point."

"I gave you the check that she gave me to give you. I recall her donation well."

"Are you still friends with her?"

"Calling us friends is a stretch. She needed my help and paid me for it. When I last saw her, she told me to get out of her house. She had lost her nose to a botched plastic surgery job. I suggested that she could make commercials like cancer victims do about the danger of too much plastic surgery."

"She didn't appreciate your advice?"

"For some, the descent from Mount Vanity is more treacherous than others. Sometimes when they fall they want to take others with them."

"The thing is that she now wants receipts for the food, and I'm not a receipt keeping kind of guy."

"I'll help if I can," Abel offered.

"Are you helping Riley since he's charged with killing a very respected man?"

"I am not his lawyer of record."

"That, my friend, is not the answer to the question I asked you," said the large man.

"Even Judas deserved a defense lawyer. Without him we would not have the Christianity we have today."

"Silas was a well-respected man," intoned McBride. "You helped me when I was charged with a crime that I didn't do and a few that I did do. If Riley is innocent, find out who was responsible. Don't just get Riley off walk and away from Silas' death like other defense lawyers like to do. You are involved and you need to find out who killed Silas. Will you do that?"

"I can do that," said Abel.

Two days later, Abel's cell phone rang. The woman introduced herself as Marsha Barnes. "Ron McBride said I should call you. I lived with Linda Garvey for over six years. She took a lot of money from me and is just plain evil."

"Can we meet?"

"Yes, but not anywhere near Center Point," said Marsha and added, "I'm only in the city for another day."

"We can meet when you want and where you want."

"Poodle Dog at 3 p.m. It's not crowded then. I think that I know who you are, but tell the waitress you are there to meet me. I waitressed there for a summer after I got away from Linda. They know who she is, and if she comes in, they'll warn me."

The Poodle Dog was a truck stop in a small town on the outskirts of Harbor City. Its menu featured large breakfasts with three-egg omelets and hash browns or pancakes. Its side order of ham steak was half an inch thick. It's an old-fashioned diner with vintage furnishings. Little had changed since the 1950s when it was last expanded.

When Abel entered the restaurant, a waitress with a tattoo of a dolphin on her wrist guided him to the back of the restaurant where Marsha was waiting. At one end of the room was an entrance to a bar with several TVs. The room where Marsha had chosen to meet was divided into two areas. One area had long tables in it, and Marsha was in the area with booths and small tables. There were also two more exits leading into a hallway to the men's and women's restrooms, and the exit leading out to the parking lot. The place where Marsha sat gave her a view of all the entrances to the dining area.

Abel introduced himself and sat down. He guessed Marsha's age could be anywhere from the late twenties to late thirties. The older Abel got, the harder it was for him to guess a person's age. She wore her hair in a moderate Afro. Her earrings were medium-sized gold hoops. She had a large backpack at her side. Nothing about her dress stood out. Her jeans and jacket were plain and not flashy. Her complexion was the color of coffee with extra cream.

"Thanks for meeting with me. Where are you headed?"

"Why do you want to know? You won't tell Garvey, will you?"

"Just conversation," said Abel. "You said that you were leaving tomorrow, so that's why I asked."

"I got a scholarship to a writing school in North Carolina. That's one reason why I agreed to meet with you. McBride said you liked to write."

"I do."

"Do you have something you've written with you? I'd like to know more about you. You don't understand the risk I'm taking by meeting with you. I haven't seen Linda for over ten years, and I'm still afraid she'll try to get back at me for running away from her. If I am going to trust you to protect me, I want to know more about you."

Abel opened up his laptop and searched his files for a few minutes. Then he turned the screen toward her so she could scroll down and read the editorial he had written recently for the local bar news.

Malice Can Kill for Generations

"Malice drinks one-half of its own poison."
…Seneca

"The statute banning firearms from courtrooms is the same statute that requires local authorities to provide lockboxes for those who carry firearms during the owner's visit to restricted areas of the building.

Hardin County simply ignores this provision of the statute, but other counties accommodate those carrying firearms. In front of one county courthouse is a sign directing those who have weapons on them to the lockboxes provided for such weapons.

Overall, I suspect that I am safer with firearms being stored in the County-City Building than if they were available to those exiting the building who might be irritated with me. Passions run high during custody cases, criminal cases, and other cases such as a property dispute, to name only a few.

Aymer Davis, a lawyer in my hometown in Iowa, was killed in 1928. He was walking home from work when a farmer on the other side of a dispute confronted him. The dispute was perhaps a foreclosure, but it may have been a boundary dispute. My cousin, Mary Ann, who is Davis' granddaughter, isn't sure. The farmer fired a shotgun, and some of the pellets lodged in Davis' legs. Davis was in front of the Post Office when the farmer confronted him with the shotgun, firing it at him. My Grandmother Di Bassio who lived in Eldora said that he fired into the sidewalk to frighten Davis, and some of the pellets ricocheted into his legs. But they could not be removed, and he died sometime after that incident from gangrene. What is certain is that his daughter, Constance,

83

heard the shot and saw him fall. She was fifteen when he died.

Constance, who I only knew as Aunt Connie, married my Uncle Carl, the brother of my mother. His widow lived in Eldora. When my Uncle Carl and Aunt Connie came in the summer for a visit, Aymer's widow would come to my grandparents' house for dinner. I only knew her as Mrs. Davis, and that my grandmother showed great deference and respect toward her. When she came to dinner, we always ate off the fine china.

Anger "feeds on raw emotions with a primal power: fear, pride, hate, humiliation. And it is contagious, investing the like-minded with a sense of holy cause," says Janne Freeman in the October 22, 2018, issue of The Atlantic magazine. Not all anger is bad. It is sometimes a great motivator for social and personal change. People preaching acceptance seldom cause great social changes.

The county's disregard of the lockbox provision of the statute is nothing that I plan on complaining to the NRA about. I may be safer because of it. It's just one of life's ironies that on a frequent basis I walk into a building seeking justice where at least one law I know about is disregarded.

Metal detectors stop weapons from entering the County-City Building, but they cannot stop the malice people carry in their hearts. That is the job of lawyers and judges. Some lawyers seem to think their job is to act as no more than a bullet to be discharged where the client points. I think the term "counselor" implies a far greater obligation.

"Malice drinks one-half of its own poison," said Seneca. Left unchecked, it seeps into the lives of many. Metal detectors have it easy. Malice often masquerades as righteous indignation, loving kindness, piety, or any other

virtue you can think of. Sometimes the worm in the soul is not even known to the carrier.

The psychologist, Karen Horney, an expert in neurosis, argued that dissatisfaction early on with your environment and circumstances is carried on for the rest of your life. The poet, Marvin Bell, wrote, "Memory is what we are." Childhood is only a small part of a person's life. If a divorce leaves a child with little more than memories of acrimony, an undercurrent of hatred of the child's parent, and long car rides on holidays, what has a divorce decree or settlement really accomplished?

There is no single answer to custody issues, and sometimes no matter how much the one side alleges malice, there really is none at all. Parenting disputes are seldom as simple as the one Solomon resolved.

The five most stressful life events according to the Holmes And Rahe Stress Scale for adults are:

1. Death of a spouse or child;

2. Divorce;

3. Marital separation;

4 Imprisonment; and

5. Death of a close family member.

Stress rankings for children are more difficult to know, and after all, rather irrelevant if you are the one experiencing the stress. Long ago I worked in a mental ward at Harborview Medical Center. I never saw a woman who was a cutter who had not been sexually abused as a child. Adults who have lost a parent in childhood have a common bond of emptiness. Some have learned to fill it better than others, but all know what it is. Children of divorced parents express similar emotions and histories.

To imagine our influence for what we do for our clients ends at the entry of final papers is folly. While we should not pretend to be mental health professionals, we can counsel our clients when what they may want could have consequences they do not want. For example, parents who constantly demean the other parent without justification while the child is growing up often find themselves estranged from the child in their later years. When a person finds out that they are not damaged goods, they also find out who gave them that message.

As a child, I learned of Davis' death, But I did not know Mrs. Davis told her daughter, Connie, that she would have to be kind to the farmer's son who was in high school with her. I learned this from her daughter, Mary Ann.

Mrs. Davis told her that the shooter's son had nothing to do with the father's death, and the son felt terrible about what his father had done. Aunt Connie took that advice to heart, so the boy knew that she did not hold him responsible for her father's death, and made sure no one else did. Aunt Connie's brother, Aymer, was a successful lawyer in Chicago.

I sent a draft of this article to my cousin to ensure that I had the facts right. In addition to offering to correct my many typos, she wrote this:

"Both Uncle Aymer and Mom were college age when the depression occurred. She became a house mother at Grinnell College which allowed for Aymer and Mom to attend college free there. Clara was an amazing woman, resourceful, full-hearted, smart, and intensely curious about everything. She loved to travel and felt that travel afforded a good education, even better than school. She was the person who did all the traveling, not her children. Mom also shared with me that across the street lived a family with a son who was a victim of cerebral palsy, and down a few houses was a youngster who today would have been diagnosed as autistic. Grandma also had playtimes set for Connie to play with these kids because she knew that

tolerance was easier to learn when children are young, as opposed to when they're older."

Ms. Davis took a terrible situation and taught her daughter how to help another person, and her helping eased much of her grief. I sometimes ask friends or prospective jurors to tell me about a life changing event in their life. I think it leads to much more insightful answers than asking what magazines they read or if they have bumper stickers on their car.

The death of her father when my aunt was in high school was a major turning point for her. She did many things. She was a teacher for many years and had two children. Her son, Tom Di Baggio, was an author and advocate for Alzheimer's research. The International Herb Association named its annual book award the Thomas DiBassio Award in his honor.

Mary Jo has devoted much of her life to helping those who are disadvantaged. She has four children. One is a doctor, one a lawyer, one a designer, and one is an executive with Amazon. Each has a zest for life that reminds me of Mary Jo when she performed high dives at our local pool. I remember the good grace and determination that her mother had when she faced her death from untreatable cancer.

Ms. Davis, by her actions and example, could have passed on to her children bitterness and a belief that life was never fair, but she did not. When counseling clients, it is folly to believe that what we are doing ends with the signing of final papers. Justice and what a client wants may not always be the same. Sometimes the best choice is to withdraw from a case, rather than harbor hatred, even if the bill is current. When advising clients and arguing in court, you must choose your words carefully. What you achieve may have results for generations."

After she finished reading, Marsha looked up over the laptop and turned it back toward Abel. "Not bad, not bad at all," she said. "I doubt many lawyers think like that."

Abel shrugged. "Some do, but many do not, or I would not have written the article."

"I wouldn't take you for a gun nut. You seem too quiet for a gun rights fellow."

"If I wasn't carrying a gun, I might have been in a lot of trouble."

"Did you shoot the guy?"

"Not for lack of trying. He ran away, and I am a poor shot."

"If you're not careful, Linda will eat you alive. She won't play by any rules you are familiar with."

"What are you going to work on while in your writing program? Is it about her?"

"She's in it. I call the manuscript *Hill Top*. It's my name for Center Point in the book. It's about growing up in Center Point and trying to make sense of the world that put Linda Garvey in my life."

Marsha pulled a few sheets of paper from her backpack. "I wrote down some things for you," she explained.

Abel read the pages, looked up and said, "Thank you. This will help a lot."

"I pity those kids if you don't get them away from her." She stood up and put on her backpack. "You've read Joseph Conrad haven't you?"

Abel said that he had.

"You don't have to travel to the Congo to travel into the heart of darkness,' she said. She looked both ways across the empty parking lot as if crossing a busy street and hurried away.

<u>10</u>

The Hardin County Public Defender's Office was located two blocks from the courthouse on the first two floors of a large building that had once been the largest department store in Harbor City. Later, it was the law school from which Abel had graduated. In the middle of its library there had once been an escalator. As Abel rode it from class to class, he imagined signs listing Torts on Floor Three, Contracts on Floor Four and so on. It had since been transformed again. In place of the five-story escalator was a large arboretum. Pleasant to look at, but also indicative of the lack of interest in renting office space in the downtown area. Since a mall was built on the outskirts of the city, business had left the downtown core. On Floor Three was the Court of Appeals, and on another floor was the Labor and Industry Office. Lawyers' offices were on other floors. The Public Defender's Office recently acquired an additional floor when crime and child dependency actions skyrocketed in step with the increase in heroin addiction, as well as the decision of the legislature that delinquent renters were entitled to free legal services. But for the legal profession and its stacks of legal arguments, now digitized rather than on paper, the building would be vacant.

The entrance to the Public Defender's Office was on Market Street, and because there were no stores on the block, parking was never a problem. Say what you will about urban blight, grief and high crime have some advantages, such as long-term investment opportunities, low rents, and lots of parking spaces.

The receptionist was a person Abel had not met before. He announced that he wanted to speak with Rosekrans. Abel was wearing blue jeans and a faded canvas work shirt from L.L. Bean. The receptionist eyed him up and down with a suspicious eye and asked if he was expected.

"More or less," he said. "We talked about my coming by."

"She handed him a clipboard with a form and told him to fill it out. She said that she would call Rosekrans once Abel returned the completed form to her.

Once upon a time, private lawyers with a nod to the receptionist, were allowed entry without explanation of where they were going. But those days were long past since 9/11. Fortunately for Abel, a metal detector was not in place, or he would have had to either announce the .38 revolver he carried in a cross draw holster or return it to his car, He preferred not to leave his gun in the car because he didn't like leaving a loaded gun in his car in case he needed it and for other reasons, such as theft.

Abel filled out the form that asked for his name, address, name of the defendant, relationship to the defendant, and the reason for his visit. He gave his relationship to the defendant as "friend," and the reason for his visit as "assisting in gathering evidence." The receptionist glanced at the form and called Rosekrans, who quickly came out of his office apologizing for keeping Abel waiting.

"You could have told me you were a lawyer," admonished the receptionist.

"That's not a card I like to play," replied Abel.

As Rosekrans got into Abel's car, Abel suggested they visit the crime scene before they went to the Medical Examiner's Office.

"Are you sure Eunnie won't mind us interviewing the Medical Examiner without telling her?" Rosekrans asked.

"I do things without asking the permission of prosecutors all the time," replied Abel.

They parked on a side street near the pergola. There was a light mist. Under the canopy of the pergola, a few people were standing close together on one end of the shelter. A street maintenance man was blowing leaves, twigs, and cigarette butts into the street gutter. Abel walked to the spot where Riley said he was sitting when Silas approached him. Over the roar of the leaf blower, Abel shouted, "Have you been here before?"

"I've driven by this spot but never stopped. I have read the prosecutor's discovery," Rosekrans yelled back.

"Rule number one of criminal defense is to visit the crime scene as soon as you can. Don't rely on others telling you what it's like."

"I've been a lawyer for five years."

"Then I must be telling you what you already know."

Glancing around, Abel saw that there were traffic surveillance cameras at the intersection. "Have you received copies of the footage from the surveillance cameras?"

"No. I didn't even know there were any."

"I'm not sure what kind of cameras those are. Most likely they are designed to catch people running a red light. But you should ask for them. Perhaps a person was driving by when the incident happened."

"If they are caught on camera, most likely they were speeding."

"Or distracted because they were watching Riley and Silas Smith. You need to request the footage from the Traffic Department. You will need to get a judge to sign off on a subpoena."

"If someone saw something, it might make things worse for Riley."

"You need to gather evidence before you decide that," said Abel.

The pergola was in front of a large white building that contained several smaller shops. On the other side of the street was a steak and sushi restaurant that was set back from the street with a parking lot as a buffer. "Have you checked with the shop owners or the restaurant to see if anyone saw anything?"

"There is nothing in the police incident reports to indicate that anyone saw anything."

Abel just shook his head and headed toward the shop on the corner. It was a second-hand clothing store that, from the looks of its display window, specialized in styles from the 1920s. The mannequins in the window were draped in dresses with fringe on the bottom. Beneath the sign on the door announcing the shop was open and all were welcome, were two smaller signs. One stated that shoplifters would be prosecuted, and the other stated that a video surveillance camera was in operation 24/7. The name of the store was Things, Things & Things.

Abel asked to speak to the manager and quickly introduced himself as a lawyer and Michael Rosekrans as the well-known Public Defender who the manager had probably heard about. The manager was a woman in her twenties with her hairstyle like something out of the musical, *Chicago*. If her name card was to be believed, her name was Ashley. She recalled seeing Rosekrans' name in the paper from some case or other, but she said that she didn't realize he was so young. Rosekrans blushed and started to say that his name was never in the paper, but Abel pressed ahead. "We are here about the incident at the bus stop. Were you working that day?"

"I heard the commotion and went to the window. The police cars and medical truck had pulled up when I looked out. I knew Silas. Everyone knew him. He didn't deserve to be beaten."

"No one does, but everyone deserves a fair trial."

She nodded, "But I don't see how I could help you."

"You have security cameras."

"Yes, but we do not discuss our security devices. That is forbidden."

"As it should. We are not interested in your security measures."

"Besides, the crime took place at the bus stop, not in here," she said.

"I suppose people come in here and are sometimes caught trying to steal a purse or piece of jewelry from the front window display?"

"Yes, that has happened."

"So, you should have a security camera or two covering the front display window that also looks out at the bus stop."

"Yes, but I cannot talk about that."

"If it covers the front display window, it should also show the sidewalk and the bus stop."

"Again, I cannot talk about that. I have been told not to," she said with a sly smile.

"I suppose the footage is retained for at least thirty days, and it's then erased unless it captured a crime in process. If so, is it preserved?"

"Have you represented someone who stole from this store?"

"Not knowingly," smiled Abel. "Can you give me the name and address of the person to whom a subpoena should be sent for the videotape?"

"I believe the police already picked up a copy. Don't they give that to the defense?"

"It has not been provided to you as of yet, has it?"

"No, I have not seen it," said Rosekrans. "This is the first I have heard of it."

"Thank you for your help," said Abel.

"Perhaps I should take your number in case I think of anything else," Ashley said to Rosekrans.

"Stellar idea," said Abel.

The Medical Examiner's Office was less than a fifteen-minute drive from the pergola, but parking was not as good. It was on an arterial street with "No Parking" signs. Even if parking was usually available in front of the building, it was taken up with demonstrators milling about and chanting. One person had set up a table in the side parking lot with T-shirts for sale demanding that the Medical Examiner, Bryan Steiner, be dismissed. One T-Shirt had his photograph on the front with blood on his hands and a caption underneath that read, "Justice for Cindy Lou Hultman."

"Who is Cindy Lou?" Rosekrans asked Abel.

Before Abel could answer, a woman with a large sign stood in front of them and said, "She was my mother. She was found in a gully wrapped in plastic and duct tape. She was beaten, and Steiner ruled that she died of a heart attack. Natural frigging cause, he said, and now the prosecutor won't do anything!"

Another woman joined them with a sign that read, "Dump Steiner." "My sister was found cut in half and stuffed in a sleeping bag. She had some meth in her system. Steiner ruled that her cause of death was undetermined because she might have died of an overdose, and her body dumped after she died. Bunch of crap! It should have been ruled a homicide until proven otherwise. Why are you two here?"

Rosekrans started to speak, but Abel cut him off. "That's private," Abel said. He stepped past her with Rosekrans quickly following him. Abel buzzed the intercom, announced who he was, and the receptionist buzzed him in without hesitation.

Dr. Steiner came from behind his desk to shake Abel's hand. He was tall and thin with a hooked nose, and his head was bald as a doorknob. Abel and he had known one another for years. Sometimes his testimony led to a conviction of Abel's client, but sometimes a verdict of not guilty. He appreciated that Abel's questions were always well prepared and designed to elicit as little doubt as he could. His court arguments never suggested that Dr. Steiner had failed to do his job in a professional manner or was negligent. Unfortunately, many defense lawyers with little else to argue about often did.

On a bookshelf behind the doctor's desk was a bronze replica of Giordano Bruno shown standing in the place where he was executed, Camp de' Fiori in Rome. Next to the statue was a bronze statue of an elongated figure standing on his head. The arms and legs seemed twisted as if trying to break free of restraints.

"That sculpture next to the one of Bruno is new," remarked Abel. "When I was last here, there were only a few protestors outside demanding that you resign. Have they inspired you to get the statue of Bruno in the agony of execution?"

Steiner sighed and nodded in the affirmative.

The doctor went on to explain. "It is a replica of a monument to Giordano Bruno at Potsdamer Platz in Berlin, Germany. Alexander Polzin was the sculptor. It represents Bruno burning at the stake while tied upside down. He was naked when they burned him, and before they burned him, they "imprisoned his tongue" by ripping it out. He was a martyr for science. He was a man I admire more and more for staying true to his beliefs. Galileo recanted his beliefs and accepted house arrest. Bruno did not."

"To be fair, Galileo had the advantage of seeing how far the Inquisitors would go to promote what they considered the common good and decency. Once upon a time, heretics were only slapped in the face. Now they get monuments," Abel observed.

"As the Medical Examiner, I can only list a few limited causes of death such as suicide, homicide, accident, natural causes or undetermined. My rulings can affect how the police or prosecutors pursue an investigation or file charges. But I don't have the final say on the charges or the end of an investigation."

"Those protesters are saying you stopped investigations," said Rosekrans.

"I know who you're talking about. The one woman had meth in her system. Not just a little bit, but a lot. Torben Korhonen, Ph.D., the toxicologist, confirmed it. Was it enough to kill her? I don't know, but she might have died of an overdose, and her body was then hidden. Perhaps to cover up the death by a drug overdose. So I ruled that the death was undetermined."

"What about the one who died of a heart attack?"

"It was clear that she died of a heart attack. Was she being beaten when she had the heart attack? Possibly. However, that is not my call."

"We are here about an autopsy you did for which you said the death was undetermined, the death of Silas Smith. The defendant, Sean Riley, is a friend of mine. I have known him a long time. Michael has been assigned to defend him. Your autopsy report lists the cause of death as undetermined."

"Usually defense attorneys are overjoyed with a ruling of undetermined. Would you have preferred murder?"

"We would like to know more. Was it an acute subdural hematoma that he died of?"

"If I knew that, I would have stated it as such. Are you asking me if the hematoma developed rapidly, or could it have come from a slow leak?"

"Yes, exactly," replied Abel.

"A subdural hematoma is a serious condition that carries a high risk of death, particularly in older people. The more rapidly it develops, the more likely it's caused by a serious injury that filled the skull cavity, crushing the brain and causing all kinds of havoc."

"Could you tell if this was a subdural hematoma that developed quickly or not?"

"No, I could not, as I suspect you already knew. What I can tell you is that the leak in the victim's brain was significant, but the tear could have happened with a small leak becoming greater. You knew that."

"I suspected it," smiled Abel. "Is it true that the cause of many slow subdural hematomas is idiopathic?"

"Correct again, counselor."

"And idiopathic means cause unknown?" pressed Abel.

"True. If I was on the witness stand, I could not confirm that Silas Smith died because of an injury at the bus stop. But the witnesses' testimony, when combined with my testimony, might lead a reasonable person to the conclusion that beyond a reasonable doubt your friend caused his death."

"That is far different from second-degree murder," said Abel.

"I try to avoid legal conclusions," said Steiner. "The cause of death is the specific injury or disease that leads to death. In this case I do not know what caused his injury. The manner of death is the determination of how the injury or disease leads to death. There are five manners of death natural, accident, suicide, homicide, and undetermined. In his case, he could have fallen thus accidentally? like Bob Saget, the actor who was found dead in an hotel room.He may have fallen, hit his head and gone to bed thinking he just had a headache. In Mr. Smith's case he could have fallen or he could have been struck. It may be that if he was struck, that the person who struck him did not intend to murder him. That is beyond what I can give an opinion on."

"In your report you said that there was some debris recovered from the back of Silas Smith's scalp."

Steiner stiffened slightly and said slowly, "Yes, some debris and some wood fibers were found. Not much, but enough to mention. It's in my report. If you look hard, you can find it somewhere in the middle of a paragraph near the end. It could be from a blow that caused his death. I cannot say with any medical certainty that a blow caused his death, but I cannot rule it out either."

"Were the trace fibers analyzed?"

"I combed it out of his hair and gave it to Detective McCoy who is leading the investigation. He and the prosecutor, Eunnie Hong, came to see me together to discuss my findings before the report was finalized."

"Is that common?"

"It is now since the protests began," said Steiner.

"Why is that?"

"I would rather not say."

"You stated there was a bruise at the back of the victim's head."

"So you did read the report," smiled Steiner.

"You said the discoloration was less than two days old. Can you narrow that down?"

"If I could, I would have, but bruises are tricky things to base a timeline on. Over time, a bruise changes color as the blood under the skin breaks down, and as the bruise heals. After forty-eight hours or so, a bruise that was red in color will turn yellow. Skin color creates different colored bruises. Mr. Silas was an African American with a fairly dark complexion. Therefore, his bruise would appear different and less pronounced than a bruise on a pale-skinned Irishman. Individuals heal at different rates."

"But if he died at the scene, would he continue to bleed once he was dead?" asked Rosekrans.

"You don't bleed after you are dead, but blood still moves around. That is how we can determine a body's position at the time of death and if the body was moved. I am not even certain that Mr. Silas died instantly at the crime scene. The paramedics attempted to revive him by giving him CPR. He may have lived for a few minutes after he fell to the ground. I opine that the bruise at the back of his head was less than two days old. That is what the literature tells me. My own opinion is that it was less than twelve hours old, but it could have been caused when he was at the bus stop."

"Debris seems like a rather unscientific word for whatever was combed out of Silas Smith's hair. Your reports are usually more specific. Off the record, can you be more specific as to what it was?" asked Abel.

"Debris was a word that Eunnie selected. She thought it vague enough to avoid confusion."

"Or perhaps create confusion."

99

"Perhaps, but I really am not certain what the debris was. An analysis of the exhibit would avoid confusion, but that is not my department. I am not going to press for one, and if anyone asks, you didn't get the idea from me that the debris should be identified. I need all the friends I can get in the prosecutor's office. Do you understand?" he asked.

The doctor glanced out to the street where a chant to fire him was gathering steam. "Perhaps you could have the debris compared to the debris at the bus stop to determine if they are similar," the doctor suggested and added, "But I suppose you already thought of that."

11

Randy Jarad shivered beneath his thin covers and listened intently for sounds from the next room where his brother, Baily, and Linda Garvey slept. Baily always slept with her, warm in the winter at the behest of her electric blanket. She always said that she was cold and liked to have Baily next to her for warmth. He had tried several times to crawl into bed with them, but she always said he took up too much room kicking and twisting about in his sleep. He didn't think that was true, but then he didn't know for sure either because he was asleep.

That morning he was glad to be sleeping alone. He waited and held his breath so he could listen. All he heard was the sound of Garvey's snoring. He slipped out of bed onto the worn carpet and tiptoed into the kitchen. The night before, Garvey had returned, she tossed his toy bat into the garbage under the sink. It was his toy, and he wanted it back. It was a gift from his father. He had used it to rap on the car window trying to wake his father up. That was until his mother pulled him away and covered his eyes. "My father gave it to me!" he cried out when Garvey tossed it under the sink. "All the more reason to not have it," she replied. She said that his father was a bad man who was too weak to live. "You need to forget him!" Garvey shouted back. Maybe she was right, but it was the only thing given to him by his father. Holding it and thinking about the memory of his father sometimes felt like a hot iron that he couldn't let go, and other times, it was a pathway for him to remember more pleasant times.

The metal door beneath the sink was stuck, and he had to jerk on it to open it. The toy bat was only eighteen inches long. A souvenir bat from the minor league father and son game they had gone to. It had only been his father and him. Baily was too small to go, so he stayed home with their mother. "Here kid, keep this always," his father said, handing it to him with a bag of peanuts. The bag was red and white, and the peanuts were still in the shells. His father had shown him how to crack the shells open and toss the husks under his seat.

Garvey suddenly grabbed him by the back of his neck and spun him around, whipping the bat from his hand. "I told you it was garbage!"

"My dad gave it to me," he wailed.

She twisted the bat out of his hand and tossed it back into the garbage. First, though, she swatted him with her open hand while spinning him around. "All the more reason to get rid of it! Do you want to be like him?"

He wanted to say yes, but he didn't want to get hit again. So he said nothing. He somehow knew, however, that he'd betrayed both his father and himself by not speaking up.

When Lori Black came to do her chores, Randy was sitting with his face to the wall with barely enough room to put a spoonful of cereal in his mouth. Both he and Baily were in their school clothes. Baily was sitting on Garvey's lap watching cartoons.

"What did Randy do now?"

"Never you mind," snapped Garvey. "But he deserves his punishment. Don't you, Randy?"

"Yes, Ma'am, I deserve it. I was wrong to disobey you," said Randy in a singsong voice.

"Say it again, with respect this time!" she demanded. Her voice was as sharp as a ruler slammed down on a kid's knuckles.

"Yes, Ma'am," he said meekly, as he did what was demanded of him.

Lori quickly started her chores. The first thing she needed to do was to check Garvey's blood sugar and give her a shot of insulin. The second was to walk the boys to the school bus stop. Lori had given up trying to tell Garvey that child care was not one of the duties assigned to her by the Korean Women's Association. However, in return for her taking on extra duties, Garvey had lessened her demands on Lori to turn over some of her pay. While they waited for the bus, Randy told her what he did and why he was punished.

"You are not supposed to talk about what happens inside the house," said Baily. "You aren't supposed to tell outsiders anything."

"It's okay, Baily," said Lori. "I'm not an outsider. I'm here five days a week."

"Mama Garvey says you are the help," replied Baily.

"She is not our mama."

"I said Mama Garvey."

Lori waved goodbye to them. Once they were on the bus, she returned to clean the house. Taking the trash from under the sink out to the outside bin was first on her list of things to do.

When Randy and Baily came home, Lori was gone, but Garvey was not alone. As they entered the house, she quickly tucked some money inside her bra and introduced Randy to Mr. Jones.

"Randy, this is Mr. Jones. He is a photographer. He says you have just the right look to be a child fashion model."

"Hello, Randy," said the man named Jones. He reached his hand out to shake Randy's hand like Randy had seen adults do. Jones was of average height and neither thin nor fat. His age was impossible to tell, but he had a strawberry colored birthmark on the side of his face that ran from the right side of his nose up and past his right eye.

For as long as he lived, Randy would never forget that strawberry birthmark. Even years after he had last seen Mr. Jones he would wake up in a cold sweat thinking that he was being pursued by that birthmark that grew larger and larger, while it attempted to catch and suffocate him. But the first time he saw it, he thought it was funny that a grown up would paint such a thing on his face.

"Mr. Jones is going to take you to his studio and take some photographs of you," explained Garvey with a great big smile.

"Can Baily come too?"

"No, sweetie pie," said Garvey. "He stays with me. Mr. Jones only wants to photograph you. He will pay me money for the photographs, and that will help me to pay bills. You want to help me, don't you? It would please me if you would help out. He thinks you are such a handsome boy that you might end up modeling clothes and maybe be a Hollywood star."

"Really?" ask Randy.

"That is what he thinks. I could be on television."

"It is possible," said Mr. Jones.

"I want to help," said Randy.

"Before taking the photographs, we can go get a Happy Meal," said Mr. Jones. "You like Happy Meals, don't you?"

"Sure," said Randy.

"Now, Randy, when you are with Mr. Jones you have to do everything he says and not back talk him."

"Everything? What if I don't want to?"

"Then just do it for me and Baily. You are the oldest man in the house, and you have to act like one."

"Okay," Randy said, and Mr. Jones took him by the hand. When they returned later that evening, Randy ran to Garvey and hugged her. Mr. Jones shook Garvey's hand, and in the palm of his hand he passed her a few bills and photographs.

"He is a wonderful lad," said Mr. Jones. "Just a wonderful lad. So well trained and docile. Thank you."

That evening under the covers of his bed, Randy began to cry and sniffle until Garvey invited him to sleep in her bed with Baily and her.

"Just for tonight. You have made me very happy," Garvey said.

"Thank you," Randy said. "Thank you."

"You are a good boy. When we talk to the counselor, you must never tell her about Mr. Jones. Do you understand? If you do, then you will be taken away from me."

"No, I promise that I will never talk about Mr. Jones. Will I see him again?"

"You will if I tell you to. Call me Mama Garvey. Don't make me angry with you."

"Yes, Mama Garvey, yes," he said, giving her a hug around her neck and clinging to her.

12

"After Bill's Celebration of Life, I'll just go directly to Johnny Burton's funeral. It's scheduled to start a few hours after Bill's celebration of life. I could stop by the house and pick you up. Are you sure you don't want to go with me?"

"Boy, you sure know how to show a girl a good time," replied Billie who was in her pajamas. They were at the breakfast table that looked out at the waters of South Puget Sound. On the water a few sailboats were already in motion. At their feet were Murphy and Barney, their two golden retrievers. They were attentively waiting for Abel to finish his bowl of cereal. He always gave them a post breakfast snack of bananas, roast beef and a few licks from the lid and cup of a Greek yogurt cup.

"It will be a nice drive. This is perhaps the last time we ever see Bill's wife and family."

"Don't go into sales, sweetie. His wife always talked down her nose to me."

"She talked down her nose to everyone. It was nothing personal. It was just part of her southern charm that made her a good prosecutor."

"I barely knew Bill and didn't know his children. I never met Johnny Burton at all."

"He was a World Boxing Champion."

"I never met him," said Billie

"He was McBride's uncle."

"And again, I never met him. You go to the funeral. I am just not interested."

Inpatient with their chitchat, Murphy knew by the sound of the silverware that Abel was done eating. He stood up and yelped for food to be put on the floor.

As Abel was leaving, Billie said, "Someone has to stay home with the dogs and count sailing ships. Besides, you like to take trips by yourself. It gives you time to daydream."

"I wonder if Penelope told Ulysses that as he went out the door?"

"Just don't miss any exits or swerve off into a ditch because you're daydreaming."

"I've never missed an exit because I was daydreaming."

Billie just shook her head because they both knew he had missed exits more than once because he was daydreaming or thinking about a case.

"I am no Penelope. You better be home tonight, or I will go looking for you." She laughed as she walked him to his car and then kissed him goodbye.

The Celebration of Life was a two-hour drive away at a country club. Billie was right; he did like to travel alone and let his mind drift. He had met his friend, Bill Harrison, over fifty years earlier on the front steps of a Catholic Church. Neither was particularly religious, but they were going through a pledge week before college started. They were staying in a dormitory where pledges stayed while they visited fraternities. The trip to the church was a chance to get out of the dorm and enjoy the fresh air. We think our lives are turned by the great wheels of fate, but in truth they are turned by the small wheels of choices and random chances. If Abel hadn't been lighting up after the service, Bill wouldn't have bummed a smoke from him. They had never met before. On the walk back to the dorm, they chatted a bit, and for the next two years they continued to chat. One day Abel told Bill that he had just gotten back from hitchhiking to the West Coast. This led to that, and they began to have coffee together which led to racquetball matches and beers afterward. Then Bill asked Abel if he would help him move a family to Annapolis, Maryland, and hitchhike back. Abel readily agreed.

The one night they spent in Annapolis they walked around the city. Near dark, Bill saw a group of Black people dressed up, heading into a church where a Hammond Porta B organ was playing. He wanted to see what the inside of the church looked like. They sat down near the back, and a man who had followed them sat down behind them. Before the preacher began to speak, a man came over to them and demanded to know if the Evil One had brought them. He wanted to know if they were believers or had come to mock their faith. Each of them assured him that they believed and wanted to be saved.

Every so often when the preacher paused, there was a resounding chord or two from the Hammond Porta B organ. People were called forth to be saved and to talk in tongues. Many came forward. A couple of young women in cotton dresses with white gloves stood near the preacher, swaying to the music and rhythm of the preacher's words. Once in a while the preacher quickly extended his hand and placed it on their foreheads. As people came forward they began to shout. Some fell back into the arms of well-dressed men with solemn faces as if they were indifferent and unmoved by the preacher's speech.

After Abel and Bill returned to Iowa City, they continued to see each other often. When Abel started a tenants' rights organization, he asked Bill to be his second in command. When Bill decided to move to Seattle, Abel moved as well. They lived together for a short time when they first moved to the Northwest. Within the first year Bill moved in with the woman he soon married, and they ended up in different cities. But they stayed in touch for birthdays. When texting became common, they texted each other during the Iowa Hawkeye games. They were close at times and sometimes not so close, mainly because they lived in different cities in different counties. Bill was a city prosecutor who handled civil cases. Abel seldom practiced in the county where Bill worked. If he did, though, he worked on cases that did not involve Bill or his office. Still, when he was in town, if possible, they would meet for lunch or coffee. They had sporadic contact with each other for many years, but whenever they met it was like time had not passed between visits. Years later after the fact, Abel learned that a foreign exchange student lived with Bill for about a year. During the last year of Bill's life, they had grown closer than when they were in college. During the time that Bill was enduring experimental cancer treatments, they spoke daily.

When Abel arrived at the country club, the parking lot was filled with late model BMWs, Volvos, Audis, and Mercedes. He parked his faded Acura at the end of the lot and hurried in. There was not much time to visit before the speeches began. Abel hardly had time to say hello to Bill's children and sisters who had traveled thousands of miles for the event. If you weren't part of Bill's family, you were most likely a lawyer, a judge, or married to a lawyer or judge who'd known Bill.

The program began with Bill's oldest son thanking everyone for coming. He was in his fifties, and Abel had seen him when he was less than a day old. The son was now married and had two children that Abel had never met until that day. He knew that he would probably never see them again. As the son spoke, Abel thought about the many things that he would miss about his friendship with Bill, even the long talks and photo updates of people Abel had never met.

Bill's oldest son related that when he was ten years old, they had moved to the Northwest. Bill had not let him touch anything until they ran to the Space Needle and touched it. It was a new life, and Bill really wanted his son to remember it. His son said that Bill was always making special events out of whatever they did. If he hadn't become a lawyer, he might have been an event planner on a cruise ship.

The next to speak was a stepson, followed by another son. Then the microphone was opened up to those who wanted to share. The first person to share was a coworker who talked about Bill's dedication to his work. At one time in their city, a truck had collided with a cast iron pergola that was on the list of national historic structures. It was much larger than the one in Harbor City and featured an underground marble restroom. The insurance companies wanted to go cheap on the restoration, but Bill had dogged them constantly. For every exception they tried to find instead of full coverage, Bill always found a flaw in their logic. Finally, the insurers were forced to capitulate and provide coverage. Even that was still not enough until a foundry had taken the job on at a loss. The coworker said that if it hadn't been for Bill's tireless efforts, the restoration would not have happened. Bill had never told Abel about his involvement in saving the historical site. Then the woman told how Bill had forced a retired federal judge to pay over half a million dollars for illegal cutting of trees just so he could have a view. Another lawyer talked about Bill's relentless dedication to passing ordinances that prevented strip clubs and rave discos from various areas of the city. Near the end of the celebration, Abel walked to the podium.

"I first met Bill over fifty years ago on the steps of a church. He bummed a cigarette from me. In later years, he said that he couldn't remember bumming the smoke from me. I don't know why. Maybe he thought I wanted it back." Abel began. Looking up at the large screen, he pointed and said, "No matter how old Bill was he was always the most handsome man in the room. He even looked good when he was bald from chemo. He had worried about that, but when his hair fell out, he even admitted that he didn't look so bad. I had to agree. He was a handsome man. Nobody here has talked about Bill being humble."

Many laughed or chuckled at that observation. Humility was not something Bill was known for. One of the coworkers talked about how he always tested his ideas against Bill who could often see the issues more clearly in five minutes than he could after a day of research. Bill was not ashamed to be smart.

"But he was humble," continued Abel, looking around the room. "He was humble without being self-deprecating. He had a good handle on what he knew and what he didn't know. He was comfortable with his place in the world as well as his friends and family. He didn't boast, but he was confident. I always admired that about him. He was not shy about dying. He simply did things well without bragging. That is a simple statement of fact.

Many years ago I was in a car accident. I was traveling fifty miles an hour and was sideswiped into a stone pillar. My head went through the windshield, and I was tossed out the driver's side door onto the pavement. My head was split open, and I lost the top of my ear. There is a good reason why they don't let accident victims have mirrors in their room. Everyone who came to see me said I looked good. Except a well-wisher who took one look at me and backed out of the room holding his mouth. He now writes science fiction. People said I looked good, but I knew that was a lie. Anyway, Bill came to see me on the weekend. He took one look at me and said I looked like Robert De Niro in *Raging Bull*. When we began to laugh about how bad I looked, I knew then that I would be okay.

I wrote this poem about our friendship. It doesn't rhyme, but I like to think that it's still a poem. It doesn't have a lot of wasted words, and it speaks as clearly as I can about my love for him."

Clearing his throat, Abel took the poem from the inner pocket of his sports jacket and read:

Poem In Memory of Bill Eugene Harrison

My friend of over fifty years is dead.
We met by chance on the steps
of a church after mass.

Chance chats on campus
led to meals at his house.
Once, we hitchhiked from Ocean City,
Maryland, to Iowa City, Iowa.

Once you have been stuck in the rain
On I-80 you never forget the friend you
laughed with.

He usually beat me in racquetball
and excelled in all other sports.
I told him about the tasty white bread
I made in a bread machine.
He described the exotic breads and
pastries
he made from scratch.

The year I took a guided river trip

through the Grand Canyon
He planned the itinerary
of a trip to Italy.

Cicero said, "Friendship improves
happiness
and abates misery,
by the doubling of our joy
and the dividing of our grief."
So it was with Bill and me

I never envied or resented
his talents or success.
Such was his grace and gentleness
that always inspired me.
I will miss him the rest of my days.

Abel shook hands with the family members who were seated in the front row. As he returned to the back of the room, a couple of people nodded at him. The poem had engendered a few laughs but at the end, the room was silent as he walked back to where he had been sitting. The program ended with Bill's sons and grandsons playing on kazoos the refrain from Woody Guthrie's "So Long, It's Been Good To Know You." Bill would have wanted everyone that he met during his life to know that it had been good to know them.

While others were settling in for another drink, a glass of white wine, or a cup of coffee, Abel hurried off. Bill had been his friend, but he hardly knew the rest of them.

He barely noticed the traffic as he hurried to the funeral of Johnny Burton. Billie was right. He did daydream while he drove. But there were no exits to miss until he arrived back in Harbor City.

They had met on the steps of a church, but no one had mentioned God or faith or even the goodness of humility. He didn't think about that until he was on the road home. Perhaps that was why the whole affair seemed somehow hollow. He was last drunk at Bill's house. He was too drunk to drive home and had crashed in a back room. In the middle of the night, he awoke and began retching into a toilet. While retching, he prayed to be well enough to drink the following evening, the same as he always did. Suddenly he realized that he had crossed over the edge into becoming a pathetic drunk.

Actually he had passed that point long ago. Oblivious to his failings, he had moved on with his life. He was like Wile E. Coyote, gone over the edge of a cliff and not realizing that he was in the air. Then he began to pray never to drink again. It was the most profound prayer of his life. Suddenly he knew that he was not alone, and he never had to drink again.

He tried to explain it to Bill, but he merely said that what had happened was explainable as a psychological phenomenon. Just because he believed it to be true didn't mean that it happened. The wife, fresh from scrubbing the bathroom, was even more skeptical of his conversion. He wondered if Saint Paul might have had a similar conversation with childhood friends. He usually took Bill's advice, but that time he didn't. In the many conversations leading up to Bill's death, they had never spoken about God or their faith. He regretted that they had not, but his faith was his, and he kept it private unless asked.

Johnny's funeral was at the Edwards Temple Memorial Church of God in Christ at 21st and Frederick Douglass Avenue It was the largest church in the Center

Point district of Harbor City. When Abel arrived, there were no street parking spots near the church. But McBride, who was on the front steps, saw him and signaled for him to park near the church in a small parking area.

"I saw it but thought I'd save it for someone who needed it."

"You needed it," laughed McBride, and he told Abel to find a spot inside.

The church was full. In the front was a large poster of Johnny Burton in his prime. He had rock hard abs and clenched fists. His casket was near the front. Beside the casket was the Olympic Torch he had carried and the World Championship belt he had won shortly after turning pro. He hadn't kept the belt long. For most of his life, he battled cocaine more than other boxers. Abel met him long after his addiction had taken him down. He didn't speak much, but he and Abel had always greeted one another with kindness and a smile.

While he waited for the service to begin, McBride found Abel and asked him to sign the boxing gloves they were going to give Johnny's son. "Thank you, my friend. Johnny always appreciated you. After the service, I want to show you something."

"What?"

"You'll see. It may help Riley, but you have to promise that you will find Silas' killer."

"I'm not a cop."

"Just do your best," said McBride.

Abel said that he would.

After the preacher spoke, the first speaker was a young boxer who talked about how Johnny had inspired him to train for hours and hours at the gym. "Because of him and other boxers who came out of the Les Davis gym, whenever a boxer was from Harbor City everyone knew they were in for a fight," the young man said.

Johnny was the number one ranked boxer in his weight class headed into the Moscow Olympics that the U.S. boycotted. Abel wondered if winning Olympic gold might have kept him away from cocaine. He doubted it, but he also wondered why Johnny, a local god, had destroyed his life in the all too predictable path of so many others. Yet like Icarus, it was his flight upwards toward the sun that the community honored; not his fall.

Icarus was the patron pagan of reckless sons and men who couldn't follow instructions. He was warned by his father, Daedalus, not to fly too close to the sun or too close to the ocean, but the son ignored the warning. Consequently, he flew too close to the sun, his wings melted, and he drowned in the sea. Johnny must have known the dangers of drugs and the life of Las Vegas for a champion boxer, but he ignored the well-worn signposts of decency. Icarus and his father escaped from imprisonment on Crete. With his fists, Johnny escaped the poverty and drugs of Center Point, but not the allure of the Las Vegas lights and dark alleys.

Unlike his friend, Bill, who worked for the city and made many contributions to the city, yet was known by only a few, Johnny was known by many, and because of his rise to fame, he affected many lives. In Wikipedia there is an article about Johnny with photographs, his wins and losses record, and a brief mention of his year in rehab. There were no Wikipedia references to Bill, yet in his quiet way, he affected as many lives, if not more, than Johnny. Heroes are needed to give average people something to shoot for, but average people like Bill were heroes in their own, quiet way. At the end of the service, Abel joined the procession of those passing by Johnny's casket. Looking at the medals aligned in the casket, he felt humbled that the man liked him as much as he did, always greeting him with a smile and a handshake.

McBride spoke last in the cleanup spot, but he only said a few words about watching his uncle train for the Olympics, and how he turned pro for the fight that earned him the World Championship. "If you are going to judge my uncle, judge him by his accomplishments. Anyone can look down on a person for his faults, but no one here has managed to accomplish what he did. He helped a lot of people and gave us all hope."

He then instructed people to walk by the casket if they wanted to. "There will be food and refreshments in the basement, after which the family will take him to the cemetery for a private ceremony."

Abel followed the crowd down the stairs and waited as the buffet line moved slowly. Off to the side, a man was testing a microphone by thumping and blowing into it until he appeared satisfied that he'd annoyed enough people for one day. "After you are settled in, those of you who did not get a chance to share your experiences with Johnny are invited to share them now."

Abel had just moved through the line when McBride found him and steered him toward a table where two stunning women in their twenties wearing gold hoop earrings were seated. They looked like they were twins. As two other men were walking toward their table, McBride shooed them away. "We got some business here. You can come back later."

"We were just sitting down," said one.

"Sit down later. We got business here," repeated McBride. He said it with a wave of his hand and a hint of menacing rage in his voice, and the two men backed away. He was a large man with large hands. When his main source of income was illegal, he had crushed the hands of many who opposed him and set others on fire with lighter fluid. In a flash, the distant past seemed ready to return.

"No problem," said one young man, pulling on the other's arm. "We don't want trouble."

"Appreciate your understanding," said McBride. "When we're done, you can sit down."

"Thanks," they replied.

"Sit down, Abel. These are my nieces, Mandy and Brandy Ryan," directed McBride.

"Pleased to meet you," said the woman he identified as Mandy. An infant sucking on a pacifier while reaching for a full breast pressing against her tight blouse sat on her lap. Abel easily understood the infant's desire for the real thing, and the young men's desire to sit with them.

"They were at the People's Park the day before Silas was attacked by Riley," McBride said. "Silas was attacked in the park."

"Did you see what happened?"

"Not only did we see it happen, we recorded it," said the woman without the child.

"Can you tell me what happened?"

"Better than that, we can show you," they said in unison.

"We heard shouting and looked up. We got most of it on video," said the woman with the infant. Her sister held up a cell phone and played the video. It showed Silas being pushed to the ground and a man hitting him. The man's back was to the camera.

"You don't have the man's face on the camera?" asked Abel. The video showed the mauling from different angles as the women rushed to the scene.

"Sorry, no. We thought that we had, but the phone stopped recording when we went over to see how Silas was doing."

"Are you sure it was Silas?"

Both nodded that they were sure. "He was well-known in the community. Everyone knew him by his suits even if they didn't know his name."

Abel asked them to play the clip again. The attacker obviously had some training. The first punch began with a twist of his hips as he gathered force with his flashing arms and a snap of his fist against the side of Silas' head. "The man had some skill," Abel noted.

"He definitely had some training. Notice how he pivoted on his toes," said McBride.

"Somehow he seems familiar," said Abel.

"I've known most of the Golden Gloves boxers for the last thirty years. I went to every state championship with my uncle. They were held at the university's fieldhouse. But I don't recognize him."

Abel asked that the video be sent to his cell phone. Before leaving, he made sure that he had received it.

"Will this get Riley off?" asked McBride.

"Not sure," Abel replied.

"Don't forget what you promised," warned McBride.

"No, I won't forget my promise or this day."

As Abel drove home past the empty stores and the houses needing paint, he felt a closer kinship with McBride and Johnny. He even felt closer to Silas who he'd never known, more so than he'd felt with any of the people at Bill's Celebration of Life. Bill and he may have been friends for over fifty years; however, he realized that their friendship, although long on events and jokes, was limited in emotional attachment. He had meant every word of his poem, but he also realized that Bill, in his heart, had always assumed he was entitled to his achievements and success. Abel had not. He wasn't raised in the same poverty and violence as McBride and Johnny. He had little personal experience of discrimination, yet he understood isolation and the sense of never belonging that Bill had never really known. He loved Bill, but he also knew that he had a deeper connection with many others. It was not enough just to defend Riley. He needed to find out who had killed Silas.

13

When Lori Black arrived for her workday, Randy was kneeling with his nose near the wall trying to eat cereal without spilling onto the floor, and Baily was in the other room watching cartoons. Garvey sat in a large chair, letting out deep sighs. She was wearing a gingham dress and a red headscarf on top of her head. If she would have had a smile on her face instead of her usual glaring smirk, she might have looked like an early version of Aunt Jemima whose likeness once appeared on pancake mix boxes before the advertising world went politically correct. There were several sheets of legal papers on the floor in front and to the side of Garvey. Some were crumpled and some were partially torn. Anything that irritated Garvey intrigued Lori.

"I should check your blood sugar level, Ms. Garvey," said Lori.

"Don't 'Ms. Garvey' me. I know you don't respect me," snapped Garvey.

"I should still check your blood sugar. I can see that you're sweating. Do you feel dizzy? Did you check your blood sugar this morning? You don't look well."

"It's because of him and his brother that I don't look well," Garvey said, pointing to the papers. Pick them up."

While Lori scrambled about picking up the papers and putting them in order, Garvey continued ranting to herself rather than explaining anything to Lori. "The useless mother and the spiteful grandmother have hired a lawyer to take the children away from me. I was served these papers last night by a process server. I asked him who he was before opening the door, and he lied. He said that he had a package for me."

"This is a lot of paper," said Lori, holding the papers up.

"Don't sass me! I am not in the mood! It was him who opened the door," she yelled, tossing a *People* magazine at Randy's back. I told him to wait but he didn't. The man knocked and like a fool, he opened the door. Then, there the man was at the open door. He said that he had legal papers for me. I told him that I wouldn't accept them, and he tossed them at my feet. I yelled at him, but he just kept walking away from me. Do you think that's legal? Don't I have to say that I accept the papers for them to be legal?"

"I suspect not, or no one would ever accept papers."

"Don't sass me, and I wasn't really asking your opinion anyway."

"I should take the boys to the bus stop."

"They aren't going to school. I need them home today."

"They need to be in school."

"Not today they don't. There is no school today. They call it a teacher training day. I call it a teacher holiday. They simply take days off when they want, and what are working people supposed to do then? Stay home with the kids that they're supposed to be teaching? It's disgraceful the things educated people get away with. How do I look? I bet you thought I was Aunt Jemima?"

"You wanted to look like her?"

"Of course, I do. Nothing white folks like better than looking down on and helping a poor servile Black woman. Aunt Jemima was her own person while men wanted her in the kitchen cooking or in the nursery looking after their brats. I'm going to see a white lawyer today, and I want his help."

"You should take your insulin, or you won't make it to his office."

"I'll be fine, and he'll help me." She held out her trembling hand. "I'll stretch out my trembling hand, and he'll help me. I'm going to a clinic that specializes in helping indigent people. Those do-gooders are the easiest to fool. They want to be fooled into thinking they're needed. And I do need him. Look at these papers! I have been betrayed by a young girl who I saved from the gutter. This lawyer has sought out people to say good things about the mother who abandoned her children. Plus, the wonderful things their grandmother has done, even though she's not seen the children for months. I helped save that young woman from the streets. She was a prostitute with a child, and I saved her and treated her like my daughter." She beat her enormous breasts that looked like they were in danger of popping. "I helped that woman. I opened my doors to her that no one else has seen for years. Yet she crept out of the dark hole she ran into and told lies about me."

Lori shook her head and kept silent while a longer torrent of words washed over her. Finally Garvey fell silent in her large chair.

"What would you like me to do?"

"Have you thought more about my offer that we split your wage?"

"I earn my money for what I do."

"The work you do for me is not hard. You could have another job and get paid before coming here. I need to hire a lawyer, and I'm in need of your help. Haven't you been listening to me? If I said that you'd stolen from me, who do you think they'd believe? Do you think that you'd ever work for them or anyone else again?"

"I need this job," said Lori. "But I'm not going to lie about my hours."

"Think on it, girl. Half of an apple is better than no apple. Now, help me get the boys ready to go downtown. I want you to drive us there and wait."

"You want me to be your driver?"

Garvey gave her a withering look and said, "You are a hired caregiver. Are you refusing to provide me care? The care that I need and the care you are being paid to provide?"

"No," sighed Lori.

"Good. Bring the insulin with you because I may need it before I come back home."

The one-story People's Law Clinic was several blocks from the County-City Building. There was a large piano displayed on top of the flat roof, a relic from the former owner who had long since gone bankrupt. Lori parked in one of the many vacant spots in front of the building. "Wait for us," Garvey instructed as she shooed the boys out of the backseat of the car.

When Garvey and the two boys entered the reception area, no one was at the front desk. On the desk was a sign, "Ring Bell for Assistance. Receptionist in Back." Garvey rang the bell several times and then sat down. In the small lobby area was a penny gumball machine. She gave the boys two pennies each, and she sat down while glancing around the room to determine if there were security cameras. She saw none but thought that one could never be too careful. She asked each boy to come over to her, so she could rub their faces clean with a napkin she'd taken from a fast food place.

From the back a receptionist appeared blowing her nose. Allergies, she said, and she blew her nose a second time, tossing a Kleenex in a wastebasket. She asked if

Garvey had an appointment. The woman had a high pitched voice with a nasal twang.

"Walk-in," said Garvey. "I need to get some advice, please."

"Criminal, civil, or domestic?" asked the receptionist. She was young and wearing trendy jeans and a designer sweatshirt.

"I'd rather talk to a lawyer about my problems than discuss them here with you."

"We have several lawyers here. Some only do criminal law. If the case is criminal, you may qualify for public assistance. The State gives us money to defend people in criminal cases. If your case is civil, like a car accident or dog bite case, there are other lawyers you can talk to. If your case is domestic, divorce or custody, then there's another lawyer here for those cases. He may be able to answer your questions."

"Most definitely domestic then," said Garvey, wiping sweat from her cheeks and patting her forehead. "I am the victim of lies and treachery when all I've done is to take these orphans into my home and protect them from their mother."

"How can they be orphans if they have a mother?"

"Half orphans then, if you want to get technical. Their father killed himself in front of the older boy, and the mother has not recovered from the shock. I took them in to save them. Now she and her mother want them back as if they were cargo to be traded back and forth as it pleases them."

"I'll get the lawyer," said the receptionist, handing Garvey a form to fill out. "Just fill out the top part where it asks for your name and address. No need to write in what your case is about."

"I need help, and these are active children!" The urgency in Garvey's voice was only a notch or two below the panic warning of an unexpected explosion in a dark mine.

"The lawyer will be right with you. His name is Samual Blount."

"Thank you. Thank you so much," said Garvey.

Samual Blount was in his early thirties with thinning brown hair already in retreat from his forehead. He had bushy eyebrows and a pale complexion as if he only got out in the sun between trips to the office and the courthouse. He was wearing a gray cardigan sweater buttoned to the top. His rather large belly extended well over his belt. He introduced himself and said, "I understand you have a problem."

"I do, I do, and so do these children. They need to be with me."

"Let's go to my office and talk. But the children should not hear our conversation. Heather, would you mind watching them?" he asked the receptionist.

"I have more things to do for the other lawyers," she said.

"It would just be for a moment or two."

"I doubt that," said Heather sarcastically.

"I have a friend who drove me here. Perhaps they could stay in the car with her while we talk."

"Excellent," said Heather.

Blount led the way to a small office that was barren of pictures and furnished with only a table and a couple of chairs. On the table was a laptop. Next to the table was a large carrying case. "This is not my office. I have an office downtown. I volunteer here, and they provide this space for me to give clients advice."

"I need a real lawyer."

"I am a real lawyer," huffed Blount. "This is just not my regular office."

"I need a real lawyer to take my case."

"We can discuss fees at another time if I decide to take your case."

"I can't afford a lawyer. I thought this was the People's Clinic."

"I give advice for free, but signing on to a case and appearing in court takes a lot of work and effort."

Pounding her chest, Garvey said, "I have only tried to help this woman, and they've accused me of trying to steal the children. You can look at the court papers. We appeared in court, and I told the court that I wanted temporary custody until Denise was capable of handling the children and raising them as a mother should. It's all here. They've now besieged me like jackals surrounding an injured lion." She slammed the packet of papers onto the table.

"Let me look at them," Samual said quietly.

He read the packet, nodding occasionally. Finally he finished and looked at her. Then he opened his laptop and reviewed the two cases. The one begun recently by Roberta Jarad, seeking custody of the children, and the one in which Denise Jarad agreed to relinquish custody of the two boys to Garvey.

Blount sighed and said, "She did give you custody. Just like you said."

"Of course, it was as I said. Do you think I would lie to a lawyer?" She shook her head violently from side to side. "No, No. I came for help because I need help. All I wanted was to help that poor child, and she has accused me of ridiculous things."

"Most of the declarations in support of the grandmother are from people who support her, but do not know how the children are doing. The law is clear that there has to be a change in your living situation, and they don't say that."

"That's good. You think they will lose."

"I think you have a good case. I do not know John Abel, but I can check around about him. I think he does mainly criminal defense."

"I am not a criminal," Garvey announced.

"I didn't say you were. I just meant to say that I don't think he's very knowledgeable about family law. Are you opposed to the mother seeing the children?"

"No, no. I've encouraged her to come see the children, but she always says she's busy."

Holding up Denise's declaration, Blount said, "She claims that you keep the children from her."

"Lies and lies upon lies, Mr. Sam. Lies upon lies. I encourage her to see the children."

"Why would she lie?"

"Maybe that's what she has told her mother so as not to look bad."

Blount nodded, "That makes sense. But what about this Marsha Barnes? She says some terrible things about you. That you tried to take her children from her. This is what she said, and he read the declaration aloud to Garvey.

"I lived with Linda Garvey for over six years. I met Linda when I was in a foster care home. My foster care mother was a friend of Linda's. Linda promised to buy me things, and I moved in with her before I turned 18. I was excited to move in with her because I had never had someone buy me things as she promised to do. While there, my son, Stephen, was also in foster care. I was a teenager but began to work on getting my son back. Linda discouraged me from doing this. My foster mom told Linda to stop pretending that she was my mother. Linda made it

128

difficult for me to get my son back. She called the social worker and lied. Finally, I did get my son back. Linda abused him and accused him of stealing things like her makeup and other odds and ends. When I tried to protect Sebastian, she assaulted me. While living with Linda, I became pregnant and had another son, Michael. Linda took him as her own and said that I had the baby for her. She told people that he was her son. She even showed people an ultrasound of Michael, and she told people it was her son. When I moved in with Linda, she applied for and got a larger apartment. We moved in right away, even though my first son was not with us at the time.

I became her home care provider but never got any of the money. Linda had it deposited into an account in both our names, but I did not have free access to the account. I later found out that I had received a lump sum payment from my deceased father, but I never got any of it. Linda closed the account and said that some money had been accidentally deposited and that she was closing the account so the money would not be taken back. She said it was her money. Then we went out and spent a lot of money on rent-to-own furniture. Linda would say to me that if I didn't do what she wanted, she would take Michael from me. One time Linda encouraged me to steal a comforter and other products. I did not do it because I realized that if I went to jail, Linda would get my children. I saw Social Security cards that were not in her name. She asked for my kids' Social Security cards so she could get housing. Later I learned there were two other young people who had lived with Linda who she had collected money for.

I lived with Linda until the year 2012. Linda drove everywhere we went. She was arguing with the State not to take her driver's license. Her blood sugar would drop so low that she would pass out while driving. This happened

*when I and my children were with her. Luckily we had just
pulled into a parking lot. Because of her weight, I had to
wipe her after she used the facilities. I think she really just
wanted to humiliate me as much as she could. Linda was in
the hospital for a gastric bypass. When she came home, I
stayed and cared for her for two weeks. Then I moved out
without telling her for fear of what she would do to me or
to the kids. Linda choked me while bending me over a car. I
tried twice to get a restraining order and was denied. She
knows how to manipulate people. I explained how she had
chased me down the road and abused my son, but the court
did not grant the order. Her conduct is so odd, it seems
unbelievable. But it is what she does. Over and over she
told me that she would take my kids. Linda qualifies for SSI
because she is bipolar and perhaps for her other physical
health reasons as well. She told me that she had kids of her
own, and they had died, but I never saw any proof of this. I
fear her to this day. I got away from her before she could
take my kids and more of my money. I am glad to be free of
her. I fear Linda will come after me someday because she
feels that she lost when I got away."*

"More lies. I don't doubt that Denise and her
mother paid her to say those things. I understand she is on
drugs. She left me in a rage after I did everything I could to
help her and her children. All lies."

"She certainly didn't hold back."

Garvey glared at him with indignation until he
glanced away from her stare. Then she went on, "Nothing
worse than the spite of a child you tried to help. I couldn't
have children and have dedicated my life to helping
others." She sounded like a preacher putting his hand on a
Bible. "I am a poor Baptist woman on disability. I get SSI
and a few dollars for taking care of the children. A powerful
woman who is against me, and who will stop at nothing has

hired a lawyer. You couldn't help me just a little, could you? I mean, if it's clear to you that I'll win, then can't you please help me?"

"I am usually only here to give advice."

"I am not an educated person. How can I possibly defend myself against a lawyer and a woman who will stop at nothing? Did you see that he even wants to see my medical records? In one of these papers, he says that he's giving me notice he's going to ask the Korean Women's Association for my medical records. Why would he want them?"

"To show that you are not healthy enough to raise the children, perhaps. I could help you for awhile. I could sign on to your case."

Suddenly Garvey began to shake and burst into tears, holding her head in her hands. "Thank you. You are my savior. I have done so much for these children and to have all my human frailties exposed in a court of law. It is like being cut open and dissected without anesthesia. All because I am a poor Black woman and tried to help children. Thank you for seeing the truth and helping me."

A few minutes later, Samual Blount opened the door of the office for her and shook her hand.

Getting into the car, Garvey said, pointing to the insulin needle, "Gimme my shot. Put it in my thigh. Put it in quick."

"You were gone a long time," said Lori.

" I got me a lawyer, and I got him for free. When the skinny white girl with no tits punked him like a little bitch, I knew that I could too. You want ice cream?"

"Yes," little Baily giggled.

Garvey laughed as the insulin raced through her veins. " Me too. Ice cream for everyone! Let's get us some ice cream at the drive-through. I feel like celebrating."

14

Abel deposited his .38 revolver into a lockbox under the watchful eye of a Deputy Sheriff and hurried down a long hall to a room known unofficially as the "Pit." In the hallway were benches occupied by out-of-custody defendants and their family, girlfriends, or friends. The Pit was a large room between two presiding courtrooms. One courtroom was devoted to sex and drug cases; the other to all other felonies. Prosecutors and defense attorneys would meet in the Pit to discuss dates for hearings, argue discovery issues, and make deals, most of all make deals. There are just not enough trial court rooms for the felonies that flesh is heir to. In the room were several tables and computer screens for printing orders to be signed by the judge. The room vibrated with a cross stream of lawyers emerging from attorney/client cubicles connected to the holding cells where in-custody defendants waited their turn to be brought to one of the courtrooms.

Abel nodded to a few of the lawyers he knew and glanced around the room until he finally saw Eunnie in a far corner with Rosekrans and Raven Oakes. From Eunnie and Raven's gestures and Rosekrans' lack of animation, Abel sensed that Rosekrans needed reinforcements. He sat down next to Rosekrans, smiled, and wished them all a good day.

Oakes' glance was noncommittal about the kind of day she wished for Abel. Eunnie's smile was more pleasant but far from beaming. Abel and she had known each other long enough to realize it wasn't a wise choice for them to treat one another rudely. Eunnie had begun in the prosecutor's office and then taken a few years off while Linder was in office. She returned when Sanchez became the county prosecutor. By nature, she favored running with the hounds. But as a defense attorney, she was tenacious in her desire to win, with or without closely adhering to the rules of evidence. At the beginning of her career, she often wore tight outfits to show off her slim figure. She preferred diaphanous blouses with dark-colored camisoles under them. When she unsuccessfully prosecuted McBride for murder, he told Abel that he regretted the case had ended so quickly. Now, a few years later, she no longer wore the diaphanous blouses, and the designer dresses were not quite so tight. Slight lines appeared at the corner of her lips, barely visible beneath her makeup. She was perhaps not a babe to a twenty-year-old, but to anyone over thirty she was still a stunner.

When Abel sat down, his unbuttoned sports jacket fell open, revealing the holster over pocket. When he realized it was exposed he pulled his jacket over it. He considered such exposure a breach of concealed carry etiquette but it had already been seen by Rosekrans

"What's that for?" asked Rosekrans, moving slightly away from Abel.

"It's for a gun," replied Abel.

"You carry a gun?" Rosekrans said with obvious amazement.

"Cops are just too heavy to carry," said Abel. "Have you ever shot a gun?"

Rosekrans shook his head. "I have never touched one and don't plan on ever touching one."

"They are often used as exhibits. You might want to familiarize yourself with guns if you're going to do criminal defense. When I started out as a lawyer, I didn't know much about guns, but one of my first cases involved the identification of bullet holes. Another lawyer and I went out to a shooting range and compared bullet holes from different caliber guns. In another case, I got an acquittal because my client was accused of using a tip-up gun, and the State's main witness claimed that he had heard the slide racketed. After my cross-examination, he had little credibility as a witness. My client had arthritis and was simply not capable of racking the slide as he had claimed.

This holster is a cross draw holster. My friend, Bill Friday, a gunsmith, recommended it because I spend so much time sitting. From a sitting position, the gun is much easier to access than if it was in my front or back pocket, or in a side holster. I recently bought it, and I'm wearing it to see if I think it's comfortable. Bill gives me a lot of good advice. We go to the shooting range occasionally, and he's helping me improve my putting groups of holes in the paper targets." Abel hesitated to tell them that his friend had encouraged him to sand and polish the interior of the poster for a quicker draw which he had done. Somehow that seemed like too much information to share or that his friend had also recommended polishing down the snap with a Dremel for ease of draw. Somehow that just seemed like too much sharing with the liberals he was among.

"Do you always carry a gun?" asked Rosekrans.

"No, but I was at the mall before I came here, and there have been shootings there recently."

"Do you have military training or militia experience?" demanded Oakes.

"No," replied Abel. "I've never shot anyone either. Not sure if push came to shove that I could, but I could at least fire a gun in the air. Gunfire alone seems to scare away most thugs."

"Carrying a gun seems risky," said Eunnie.

"Perhaps, but you never know when you might need one. You can't depend on finding a wrench laying around to save yourself or some damsel in distress."

"No, I suppose not," smiled Eunnie. "As if that would ever happen in real life."

Years ago she had stripped nude like the Venus de Milo. She was tied to a pole while her captors played casino to decide if she would be gutted or have her arms cut off. She thought that she was modeling for an erotic photo shoot, but the card players' plan was to make a snuff film. Abel had barged in with a wrench and saved her. For various reasons, the incident was kept a secret. "As if that would ever happen in real life," she repeated.

"As if," said Abel, returning Eunnie's smile.

"I can't imagine what you would do with a gun other than shoot your foot off," scoffed Oakes.

"No need to insult Abel," snapped Eunnie. Turning to Abel, she added, "We don't need a lesson on guns and holsters. What I need to know is what you are doing here, Abel."

"I am consulting with Rosekrans on the case."

"So, you are the cause of the problem. I wondered where he got the idea of subpoenaing the videotape from Things, Things & Things. It will get you nowhere."

"Seemed like a simple discovery request," said Abel. "After we've seen the videotape, we can decide where it takes us."

"McCoy already had the videotape, and I quickly reviewed it. The processing took some time, and I've given it to Rosekrans, but he still wants the judge to sign the subpoena."

"As I said, I think that getting it directly from the source rather than having a copy made by the police is best.

This way I won't worry about possible editing," said Rosekrans.

"Are you accusing the State of altering the videotape?" snapped Eunnie.

"I prefer to think of it as helping the police and prosecution avoid unnecessary accusations," smiled Abel.

"You were the one who said the police were processing the videotape. What does that mean?" asked Rosekrans.

"Just an expression," Eunnie replied. "I wanted to get this case over with, and I made a good offer. If you want to try and stretch this out, I can withdraw my offer. The videotape from Things, Things & Things doesn't really help your client," declared Eunnie. "There's a glare on the window. It shows Riley quickly getting up and Silas Smith falling backwards. It is consistent with the statements of the witnesses."

"I bet it doesn't show Silas Smith's head hitting the ground," noted Abel.

"That part is obscured by the bench and the dark plexiglass," said Eunnie. "We can't see what happened on the ground."

"Nor does it show me slamming him into the cast iron supports of the bus stop,' said Riley.

"Being with Abel has made you feisty. That can easily be explained by the glare on the window."

"All I want is what's best for Riley," said Oakes. "And I'm not convinced that either Mr. Rosekrans or Abel want what is best for Riley. I think a litigation guardian ad litem needs to be appointed to assist Riley."

"A what?" asked Abel.

"A what?" echoed Eunnie.

"You heard me. He needs a neutral lawyer who will look out for his best interests. I am afraid that you are leading this young lawyer astray, and Riley might receive a long prison term because of your arrogance and poor advice."

"Or are you afraid he'll be released to the streets, and you'll have to find him housing? If he's in prison, will you still collect your monthly fee as his V.A. payee?"

"That is a despicable accusation," huffed Oakes. "I am his guardian and have his best interests at heart."

"I have his best interests at heart," said Rosekrans.

"He should be evaluated for competency before either a trial or an agreement is reached," said Abel.

"Sounds like a stall tactic," said Eunnie. "You know very well that an evaluation may take months, and nothing can happen in court until the evaluation is completed."

"Oakes became his guardian because he was adjudged mentally unfit to take care of himself. He should be evaluated," said Abel.

"I have an order prepared to transfer him to a state hospital for observation and evaluation," said Rosekrans.

"How convenient," sneered Eunnie.

"The delay is needed anyway for you to evaluate the videotape," said Abel.

"I told you that I've already reviewed it," said Eunnie.

"I mean the second video. The one in the park where Silas Smith is attacked," said Abel.

"I don't know what you are talking about," protested Eunnie.

"What video?" asked Rosekrans.

Holding up his smartphone, Abel said "This one." He held the phone so all could look at the video.

"I've not seen this before," said Eunnie. "How did you get it?'

"It was delivered by the maker of the video to the police station about a week ago."

"Why haven't I seen it?" demanded Rosekrans. "I don't have it. It's not in my possession. If the police have it, they've never sent it to my office. If it were, I would know about it."

"Little cricket ," began Abel with a shake of his head and a slight sigh and a tsk from his lips. "The prosecution only has to turn discovery in its possession over to the defense, even that which helps exonerate the defendant such as this video does. If the prosecution hasn't received the evidence, it doesn't have to provide it to the defense." Able paused and pointed a finger at Eunnie. "Eunnie, after McCoy showed you the video, did you tell him to stick it in a filing drawer and forget about it?"

"I have not seen the video, and you can't prove that I did. I do not like your accusation."

"I suppose you do not, but that does not make it true. No text or email messages between you two? That's wise because you can never tell when a clerk might unknowingly provide incriminating evidence in a public disclosure request," said Abel.

"The video is useless. The incident happened on a different day than the day your client assaulted Mr. Silas. What does the video really show? A man wearing gray pants and a pink shirt was involved in an altercation with Mr. Smith? There isn't one shred of evidence that Mr. Smith was injured in that incident or that it's related to his death."

"You sure know a lot about this video for never having seen it before," mused Abel.

"Rosekrans, I will offer your client negligent murder in the first degree. He'll be out in twenty months," said Eunnie

"I don't think so," Rosekrans responded to the offer.

"Last week you were begging me for manslaughter with a sentence of eight years."

"Things change," said Rosekrans, standing up. "Things change." Later, as Abel and Rosekrans were walking out of the courthouse, Rosekrans asked, "Would your friend Bill mind if I tagged along to the shooting range with you?"

"I don't think he would mind at all. I know I would not,' replied Abel. "He is a good friend. We have lunch on Tuesday's. He is a craftsman his fingers know more than I do about a lot of things. He did two tours in Viet Nam. He volunteered to jump out of airplanes, but he thinks I am foolhardy for not having a CCTV for the front porch of my office.

"Why is that?"

"My front door doesn't have a peephole or side windows. He thinks my office is in a bad neighborhood and I need to know who I am opening my door to."

15

Abel entered the courthouse by way of the employee/ lawyer entrance, showed his Bar ID card, and was waved on by the security guard. Near the entrance was an espresso stand. Next in line behind a woman who couldn't decide between a twelve- or sixteen-ounce latte made with whole milk or two percent milk stood Laconia Jones. He wore his police blue sergeant uniform with chevrons on his sleeve denoting his years of service. He had broad shoulders and a waist that was not quite as narrow as when the chevrons were sewn on his sleeve. He was sergeant of the Harbor City homicide unit. On the days when he was not the lead detective on a case, he either lifted weights or ran ten miles. Usually he was dressed in plain clothes consisting of shoes with rubber soles, a shirt and slacks that he didn't mind if they got spit on, pitted out from running, tramping about a crime scene, or sweating long hours while on a stakeout. He never wore a tie because he considered them useless and more trouble than they were worth. On his hip was a standard issue Beretta automatic, and on his ankle was an Airweight S&W .38. He was grateful for the backup weapon, even though he had seldom used it while on duty.

"Laconia, I didn't recognize you," said Abel.

"Uniforms make us all look alike," laughed Laconia.

"Are you off to a parade? If you were being given an award, I'm sure one of your ex-girlfriends would have told me."

"None of the above," laughed Laconia.

They had been friends for many years. Until a few years ago, they had eaten breakfast together and played golf every Saturday morning. When one of their foursome developed cancer and died, Laconia bought a motorcycle and said his interest in golf had ended. But they still ate lunch together as often as they could. The joke of the foursome was that Abel, as their token white guy, could get them into golf courses from which they would otherwise have been barred.

After the woman ahead of him opted for orange juice and a muffin, Laconia said, "I'll have a venti-nonfat latte with three shots of hazelnut."

"One Laconia coming up," said the barista.

"They named a drink after you?" asked Abel.

"You're Laconia," beamed the barista. "I'm new here, and that was one of the drinks they taught me to make. I didn't think anyone would ever order it, but here you are."

"Here I am," Laconia agreed.

"One Laconia," she said to the woman working the espresso machine.

"Here it is," said the woman, placing the tall cup in front of Laconia.

"I saw you in line, and I already started making it while the juice and muffin lady made up her mind," she explained.

They stepped away from the stand and found a quiet corner of the lobby.

"So why are you wearing a uniform?"

"Eunnie Hong," said Laconia, rolling his eyes. "She must have attended some seminar for prosecutors and came back with the idea that police officers should wear uniforms when testifying. She said it would make us more credible with the jury. I was on the stand at the end of the day yesterday, then called back to finish up this morning. I don't think that I'll be wearing a uniform for any more trials, though." He grinned and took a long pull on his latte.

"What happened?"

"This is a murder trial with two defendants. Calvin Green is the defense attorney for one of the defendants, and a new public defender, Mike Rosekrans, is counsel for the other one. Calvin began his cross by asking me why I was in uniform rather than in plain clothes. I couldn't resist telling him that I was told my testimony would be more credible if the jury saw me in a uniform."

"You said that? Eunnie must have lost oxygen objecting."

"She was not happy. Calvin couldn't leave that bone alone and gnawed on it for as long as he could. Later, Rosekrans tried to do the same, but the judge cut him off. He is a feisty young lawyer."

"I've met him."

"We talked on break. He said that he knew you, and you were taking him out to a shooting range."

"He seems like a nice fellow with potential to be a fine lawyer. He is eager to learn and a bit naive. He reminded me of myself when I was just starting out." Abel glanced at his watch. The Jarad/Garvey hearing was more than a half hour away. He'd already made an outline of his argument and reviewed the file the night before. "So, how are you and McCoy getting along?"

Laconia shook his head and sighed. "I was glad when he transferred over to the County Sheriff's Office, and I wasn't overjoyed that he came back. We don't interact much. He's been doing this for a while, and the less I have to work with him, the less I can be blamed for anything. Eunnie wanted him back in the department. They have similar ideas about what is good police and prosecutor cooperation. My captain and lieutenant weren't in favor of his return, or at least they were in favor of pissing Eunnie off."

"He sat on the video that I had the Ryan girl deliver to the police station. I told her to ask for you."

"I wondered about that. She said that she was told to give the video to me. I wasn't involved, and now I am somehow involved. Thanks. This was your doing."

"Have you figured out who assaulted Silas Smith in the park?"

"Not yet, but we have some leads we're working on."

"I think I know who it was."

"Who?"

"Let's have lunch at the Parkway, and I can explain why I think that I know who it was."

Laconia glanced at his watch and said he would be there by 12:30.

The courtroom where Abel's hearing was being held was a large courtroom. It was sometimes used for jury assembling and swearing in of judges and new lawyers. Most of the time the back twenty rows of gallery pews were empty. When Abel entered, Blount was seated at a bench in the far back waiting for Abel while looking at his notes.

"Are you John Abel?" Blount asked.

"Yes," Abel replied, and asked Blount who he was.

Blount introduced himself and added, "A mutual friend of ours, Steve Edgington, described you."

"Hopefully not in unflattering terms."

"No. He just said you have very white hair, a short gray beard, and you would be carrying an old briefcase. Can we talk in the hall?"

"Sure, but let's tell the judicial assistant that we're here, so our case is not stricken."

"Good idea," said Blount. "I'll wait for you."

Roberta Jarad and Denise Jarad were seated on a bench near the area for lawyers that was marked off by a railing and swinging gate. On the other side of the aisle sat Garvey. She was wearing a black dress, a small hat held in place with a large ebony hatpin, and white gloves. The last time she wore that outfit was at a church attending the funeral of a man from whom she'd hoped to inherit some money. When she saw Abel stop to talk, she leaned ever so slightly closer in an effort to hear what was said, but she still couldn't overhear.

Abel followed Blount into the hallway. "Edgington said you had been in practice for a while."

Abel nodded but said nothing.

"I haven't seen you down here in the family law court before."

"I have a general practice. Criminal law takes up most of my time, but I do other things as well. I dabble in many things. Jack of all trades, master of none. That's me," smiled Abel.

"If we argue your motion and you lose, your client will owe my client for my attorney's fees. I wondered if you might not want to cut your losses now and agree to dismiss."

Abel shook his head. "I think the declaration from Marsha Barnes is powerful, and I have additional declarations that support the Jarads' desire to take custody away from your client."

Blount shook his head. "You have a high hill to climb. You have to show there has been a change in circumstances in the home of my client to warrant the court even considering taking custody away. Did you read the declaration of the counselor? I filed it yesterday. If you want to continue the hearing to consider it, I am not opposed to that." He handed Abel the declaration to review

144

as if he doubted Abel would really read it. He thrust it at Abel as though it was of exceptionally great importance.

The declaration was written by Debra Cowlitz, a certified family and mental health counselor, with a master's degree in counseling.

"I, Debra Cowlitz, do hereby swear under the laws against perjury that the following is true and accurate. I am a licensed family and mental health counselor at LAKESIDE CHILD AND FAMILY COUNSELING, LLC. I am writing with regard to the therapeutic treatment and care of Baily Jarad and Randy Jarad. They have been in treatment with me at Lakeside Child and Family Counseling, LLC, for six months.

Both children have treatment goals related to overcoming the trauma resulting from their biological family. They will continue to receive treatment with me for a long time to come.

In their best interests, I recommend no further contact with this biological mother or her adoptive mother or their grandmother due to physical, mental, and emotional abuse of these children. This abuse resulted in the loss of the children by the biological mother, and they are now under the legal custodial care of Linda Garvey. It is my hope to continue treating these two children and help to repair this damage."

"That is one powerful statement," emphasized Blount. After a dramatic pause, he added, "I have counseled my client and advised her that the mother should, in time, have visitation with the children. Ms. Garvey does not and never has wanted to break the bond between the mother and her children, but they need time to heal. If you dismiss the case, she will voluntarily work to reestablish the family connections. But if you persist in pursuing this case, then she'll do what is best to protect the children because their

145

mother clearly does not have their best interests at heart. The grandmother is old. She cannot care for the children, and the mother has mental issues."

"Old skin can conceal a lot of life. I think we should just go make our arguments," smiled Abel.

"But you will tell your clients about my offer?"

"Of course," said Abel.

"I know this commissioner. He is very serious. Do you know him?"

"Ever so slightly."

"He does not take kindly to motions that waste his time. The mother has mental problems, she gave up custody, and the grandmother is old."

"I have heard that," said Abel. "I have served declarations that support my clients. I have the declaration of Marsha Barnes."

"She is an ungrateful drug addict who hasn't seen Linda Garvey in years."

"There is a reason why she has not seen your client in years. There is a more recent declaration that says your client just wanted the children for their SSI money."

"So, no point in trying to resolve this on our own?"

" I never said there was."

There were several cases ahead of them on the docket, and they were the last to be heard when Commissioner Edmond Goldman called the case. He was in his fifties and pale skinned as if he seldom got out in the sun. "Mr. Abel, long time since I saw you." Placing his hand over his microphone, he added, "Will all your clients be keeping their body parts intact?" At his own joke he chuckled softly. To Blount he said, "Last time Abel was before me he had a client with a prosthetic nose. She pulled it off at the end of the hearing."

"I had nothing to do with that," smiled Abel.

"So you said," laughed Goldman. "Well, what do you have for me today?"

"This matter involves two cases. In one Linda Garvey is the petitioner, and the Roberta Jarad is the petitioner. I represent Roberta Jarad. I am asking that adequate cause be found on Roberta Jarad's petition that the she granted visitation with her grandchildren pending a trial on the matter." Explained Abel.

"I am asking that no adequate cause be found, for this petition to continue and that the case be dismissed and the grandmother be denied visitation," said Blount.

"I have read the files. I have read everything that has been submitted. Mr. Abel has two separate cases. If I dismiss the mother's petition, the grandmother's case could still proceed."

"I would ask that it be dismissed," interjected Blount.

"We can get to that. Mr. Abel, what is the change in circumstances that warrant reopening the mother's claim for return of the children?"

"Ms. Garvey induced my client into signing custody rights over to her on the ruse that she would teach my client how to be a better parent. I have had the court transmit the records from the day that the custody order was entered."

"I've read it."

"Clearly, it was intended that Ms. Jarad live with Ms. Garvey. That has not happened. What has happened is that she has been barred from the home. A parent always has a right to seek the return of his or her child. Being a parent is one of the most fundamental rights anyone can have."

"What do you have to say about the declaration of," Goldman paused and leafed through the court file until he found the declaration, "the declaration of Debra Cowlitz? What do you say in response to it?"

"It stops visitation," interjected Blount. "I believe in my client so much that I have taken on this case for free."

"That is admirable. You will have your turn," said the commissioner.

"Debra Cowlitz declaration is just a conclusory statement," said Abel. "I don't know what the basis is for her conclusion. She has never met Denise Jarad or Roberta Jarad. Ms. Garvey could be influencing the children to say whatever she wants them to say. She persuaded my client to give up her parenting rights. More importantly, I am not sure why the children were seeing a counselor in the first place. As an additional matter, I want to further explore the health of Ms. Garvey."

"Why is that an issue?" demanded Blount.

"It goes to the heart of whether she can be depended upon to care for the children. She is obese, has high blood pressure, is diabetic, and may be bipolar. Denise Jarad, was her caregiver because she needed assistance to take care of herself. Denise was paid by the Korean Women's Association. We have a situation in which Ms. Garvey claims to be healthy and well enough to care for children. But she is sick with obesity, bipolar issues, and diabetes. I want to explore that. It sounds like she has developed the high art of conning the system to a new level. She claims she is in poor health when she wants assistance from the state but in this court, to you, she claims to be healthy and well enough to take care of two small children. She is a game player who is out for herself and only for herself."

"I object to that characterization," said Blount.

"I just learned about Ms. Cowlitz. I am curious why they have been seeing a therapist. I will want to send out a notice to the health care provider. That will take some time."

"Mr. Abel did not want a continuance when I offered it to him, and he should not have one now."

"I don't want a continuance. I just want to proceed with my discovery."

"Enough," said Goldman. "I am ready to rule. I agree that there is adequate cause to proceed on the petition to grant Denise Jarad custody of her children. I do not have to rule on the merits of the petition of Roberta Jarad. Mr. Abel proposed a gradual increase in visitation for the mother and grandmother. The declaration of Debra Cowlitz is long on opinion but short on facts. Nevertheless, I will order that the first two weeks of visitation with the minor children shall be in a public place. Mr. Blount, when you have more, you can bring a motion for me to consider. In addition, I am appointing a guardian ad litem to investigate the claims of the mother, and to report back to the court on what is in the best interests of the children. Mr. Abel, your clients will be responsible for the initial retainer for the GAL. That will be all for today."

"Could I be awarded attorney's fees for today? My client is indigent."

"No. You said that you were working for free. I won't change that," said the commissioner.

"Thank you, Your Honor. I'll prepare an order," said Abel.

Garvey had arrived at the courthouse with the two children and Lori Black. Prior to the hearing she told Blount that she wanted the commissioner to see how devoted the children were to her. She also wanted him to bring to the Court's attention that what Denise and her mother were doing was tearing the kids apart. Blount, in a rare display of backbone, convinced her that bringing the

149

children into the courtroom would work against her. He told her that the last thing a family law commissioner wants to see are children in the courtroom hearing about the case. Blount emphasized that the best way to lose custody was for the commissioner to sense that Garvey was manipulating the children. Reluctantly, Garvey agreed to keep them out of the courtroom, and Blount showed her a small conference room where Lori Black and the two boys could wait.

No sooner had Blount and Garvey entered the small conference room than Garvey burst out, "I just know the commissioner should have seen the boys with me. If he had seen little Baily on my lap and Randy pressed next to me, he would have ruled differently. I know he would have."

"You don't know that," said Blount. "I have been doing this for a while, and I know what I am doing."

"Seems like that Abel fellow has been doing it longer and knows more about what he is doing than you do," snapped Garvey. "The judge hardly let you speak."

"It was a commissioner, not a judge."

"Whatever. You said it would be over once he saw the statement of the counselor, Ms. Cowlitz. She wrote what you said you wanted. She could have written more, but you told us that what she said was just fine."

"It should have been," said Blount.

While they were speaking, Baily crawled into Garvey's lap, and Randy stood next to her with his head on her shoulder. "I'm hungry," said Baily.

"You'll eat soon," said Lori.

"I decide when they eat," said Garvey.

"The commissioner appointed a guardian ad litem to investigate the case. There is a good chance he will recommend that the children stay with you," said Blount.

"Why is that?"

"Because they are with you now, and the mother gave up custody," replied Blount.

"The case should have ben thrown out. It should have been dismissed."

"I am not surprised that the commissioner found that there was adequate cause to go forward. She had a declaration from a priest and even a retired judge or two and and many other declarations about how good a person the grandmother is."

"You said it would be over today."

"I said it might be over today. I promised to help you through this hearing."

"Mister Sam, you're not going to abandon me now, are you?" Garvey said, with a hand on her breast. "They have money and a lawyer on their side. I am alone in the world trying to protect these children. I gave them a safe home when no one else would. The mother did not go to her mother for help. She came to me. She came to me," she repeated. "If there wasn't something wrong with the grandmother, why would she come to me? You have to help me. You have to defend the children. They have to stay with me."

"I want to be with you," said Baily.

"I will protect you," said Garvey. "I will protect you if it takes my last breath."

"I love you," said Baily. "I'm hungry. Can we eat soon?"

"I'm hungry too," said his older brother.

"There is a McDonald's near here."

"I don't have enough money to afford McDonald's," said Garvey. "They can wait till we get home. We can have butter and jelly sandwiches."

"It will be my treat," said Blount.

"You don't have to do that, Mister Sam."

"I insist," said Blount. "You boys like Happy Meals, don't you?"

"No!" shouted Randy, shaking his head. "I don't want no Happy Meal."

"You don't have to get a Happy Meal," said Blount. "You can have what you want. They have hamburgers, cheeseburgers, and fries."

"I don't want a Happy Meal."

"Never fear, Randy," said Garvey, putting her arm around him and pulling him close to her. "Never fear. I will stay close to you."

With gratitude in his eyes, he smiled up at her.

"You have to help me save these boys, Mr. Sam. They need me."

"I will," said Blount. "I will."

16

The Parkway tavern was a neighborhood watering hole two blocks from Abel's office. It was a neighborhood waterhole with lots of old wood and televisions always dialed into several sporting events. It was one of the few bars in the city to have on tap Heidelberg, a locally brewed beer favored by many over the more exotic and costly craft beers. The Parkway served what many considered the best hamburgers in Harbor City and had several pool tables in a back room.

The part owner and main waitress was Sally Grimes. Many of her customers she knew by name, and all of the regulars she knew by what they ordered. She always wore a knit cap, colorful knee-high socks, and bowling shoes upon which she glided about the bar and front room with the grace of an athlete.

Abel arrived early ahead of the noon crowd and slid into a booth. He opened his laptop on the table. Sally nodded at him and brought him a Steelhead root beer and a glass of water.

"Ready to order or will you scan the menu before ordering your usual?" she teased.

"I'll wait for Laconia before scanning the menu and ordering the usual," he responded. "Let me know if you want me to move to a smaller table."

She flipped a coaster on the table and said, "You're fine, Just don't be starting any fights with younger, bigger, or faster fellows, and leave the others alone just to be safe."

"I think that eliminates everyone in the room," said Abel.

"My point exactly," she said with a wink as she walked away.

Abel enjoyed the Parkway. It reminded him of the many bars he had frequented when he was drinking, neither too low nor too high in the social order of life. At the bar and scattered about the room were a few men in suits and ties, but most of the men wore jeans and flannel shirts with suspenders spread well apart by ample bellies. He had gone to the University of Iowa where across the campus were several bars. One bar, the Airliner, was always crowded with fraternity boys and sorority girls always dressed in the latest of fashions. Around the corner at Joe's. the college kids who lived in dormitories hung out. Farther away at the Mill Restaurant, the writers and art students gathered. He never felt comfortable with any of the groups and favored the bars far away from the main streets where the booze was cheaper. There the rooms were filled with men and women who gathered to share a drink, and not talk about either their hopes or failures. In one such bar, he often met the women with whom he betrayed his first wife. It was after one such meeting fell through he had written this:

Problems of a Deferred Rendezvous

At a restaurant table a young
man stabs his watercress.

She is late, very, very late
past his remaining.

The rage.
The rage.

The watercress is perforated
and not even his wife
to complain to.

Why he was such a loser at that time he had no idea. He thought the poem was good when he scrawled it on a bar napkin. Now he thought it was no more than a pathetic cry for help from a man who did not believe in salvation. All he gained from his bad conduct was more isolation and self-loathing. He was raised with better values than the ones he practiced. His first wife's greatest fault was that she loved him, and he could not forgive her bad taste and poor choices in men. Over time, he figured out that so many of the faults of their world that he railed against were simply his own faults and undeserved pride. Since then, he had made his amends to her, and she had forgiven him. He had not seen or heard of her in years. They say in AA that, in time, you won't regret the past or wish to shut the door on it. Well, he was still waiting for that part about not regretting the past, but it was not one that he had any desire to drink over either. It kept him humble to remember his past and not wish to repeat it ever again.

Laconia was delayed and Sally slid him another Steelhead onto his table without him asking. He liked the root beer. It was not overly foamy and did not have a bitter licorice taste as many root beers brewed in small quantities often did.

He stared at his laptop and watched the video of Dalton attacking Levi in the parking lot of the YMCA. When Abel interviewed Dalton, Dalton went out of his way to control the conversation. He wanted to show that he was smarter than Abel, and he was the victim of an attack by Levi. He said several times that he was used to discrimination. He was a mixed race Jew, and he knew how things would go down if the police showed up, and he had a gun. Abel didn't argue with him. There was no point in that. He merely listened. Levi lunged awkwardly forward in the video, and then he retreated into a mainly flat-footed

155

defensive position. Dalton moved in on the balls of his feet and unleashed a solid cross into Levi's temple, sending the slower man reeling. It was all over an alleged ding of Dalton's BMW that Abel was never even allowed to see. The prosecutor opposed it, and the court later ruled that the ding, if there was one, on Dalton's care door was not related to the alleged assault of Levi on Dalton, even though it was what had started the whole affair.

Dalton carried rage on his shoulders like some carry a coat. Abel had done some research on him. Before the incident with Levi, he had challenged a school crossing guard who told him not to park in a no parking zone. While Abel waited for Laconia, he first watched the videotape of Silas assault in the park, and then the YMCA videotape of Dalton attacking Levi. . He watched the tapes several times. Every time he watched the videotapes, the more convinced he was that Dalton had assaulted Silas Smith the day before Riley was accused of assaulting him. Prior to striking Levi in the temple, Dalton had shifted to his left while cocking his right arm. After quickly striking and bouncing out of range, he struck again. The Dalton's movements were identical against his victims he outclassed, like a orca with a seal.

"This isn't a study hall. If you're done with the booth, I'd like to sit down," said a young man Abel had not seen before. While he was studying the videotapes, the bar had filled up, but there were still some unoccupied tables. "We'd like to sit down," repeated the young man, resting his palms flat on the table and bending down eye-to-eye with Abel. He was wearing a blue blazer and a dress shirt without a tie.

"My friend will be here soon," replied Abel.
"We are here now."

"So you are," smiled Abel. "Are you asking to join me?"

"That is not what I am asking," said the man. Behind him a woman pulled on his arm.

"Do you normally walk down dark roads without a flashlight?" Abel asked, closing his laptop.

"We can sit at another table," the young woman whispered, pointing at a long table with high stools and space for people to stand and eat.

"Not very private. So could he."

"Pardon me," said Laconia, edging into the booth. With his wide shoulders, he took up far more than half of his side of the booth.

"Sorry, I'm late," said Laconia. "But I see you're making new friends while I was away." He smiled at the young man and introduced himself. "I'm Detective Jones with the Harbor City Police Department, but if you're a friend of Abel's, you can call me Laconia," he said, extending his large right hand. There were several scars on his knuckles.

"We'd better get to that table before it's taken," said the woman.

"Yes, we should," said the man, retreating backwards.

"I can't leave you alone," smiled Laconia. He waved at Sally who nodded. After a circuit of the room taking orders and collecting money, she came over to them and took their orders.

"Cheeseburger and a salad without dressing." Laconia gave her his order.

"I know, separate plates for your food," said Sally. "And for you?"

"Cheeseburger with salt and vinegar chips."

"Same plate okay?" She smiled.

157

"Preferably," nodded Abel.

"I have to be back in court this afternoon," said Laconia. "So, tell me what you know. You said that you know who attacked Silas Smith."

Abel turned his laptop toward Laconia and played the two videotapes. "Benis Dalton is the fellow who attacked my client in the YMCA parking lot. The moves are the same."

"He moves like a guy with some boxing training. Lots of guys move that way. Moves on the balls of his feet, then shifts to the right, moving in and out. Not really signature moves."

"Isn't there a CCTV video of what happened in the park?"

"No such luck. As a compromise with BLM and the ACLU, the city took down its cameras in the park. They were deemed intrusive." Laconia shrugged. "Personally, I don't think it is a bad thing to be intrusive when it comes to drug dealing in the park, but no one contacted me."

"What about CCTV in the shops or at the street intersections?"

Laconia shook his head. "There were some shops that have CCTV and some of the intersections do, but they are erased every 7 to 30 days depending on protocol. The tape of the assault in the park was well past that date."

"So you don't think you can tie Dalton to the assault? No luck in canvassing the area to see if anyone remembers him?"

Laconia shook his head. "Your video in the park was taken a day before Riley pushed Silas."

"Subdural hematoma's can take awhile."

"I have asked all the people there are to ask."

"Perhaps you have been asking the wrong people. You haven't asked me or McBride," said Abel.

158

"Burger with salad on separate plates," said a man wearing a chef's apron and a hairnet. Laconia raised his hand, and the man set the plates down. Moments later he returned with Abel's plate and silverware wrapped in a thick white napkin. The knife was a steak knife, and the burgers were thick and piled high with tomatoes and lettuce. They each cut their burger in two, and Abel began to eat while Laconia stared at him.

"What about you and McBride?"

"I talked to Dalton that day, not long before the assault."

"So why waste my time on a video?"

"I thought a little building of the suspense a good thing. Besides, I think you are wrong about discounting the similarities in the boxing technique."

"Even if Dalton did hit Silas Smith, it was still the day before."

"The blow to Silas Smith's temple may have caused a subdural hematoma. Those things can be slow acting. If not treated, the leak in the soul cavity will get bigger over time. That may have been what happened to Silas Smith. You will need to talk to people and find out if he complained about headaches or blurred vision."

'I can see how this might help Riley, but it won't please Eunnie. She likes to have simple. The simpler things are the easier it is to get a conviction. This may get Riley off the hook, but Dalton will point the finger at him anyway."

"I prefer not to be involved in this,"said Abel.

"Little late for that, Bubba. If you are a witness, then I will name you as a witness."

"I would prefer the title unnamed source."
Laconia shook his head and bit his lip. He finally said, "You are sadly a confidential source. I can't keep you

159

secret any more than I would agree to the planting of evidence at a crime scene. That may be McCoy's specialty, but it is not mine."

"I think returning evidence to a crime scene is different from the planting of evidence."

"We should not be talking about this. We both know the ice pick that killed Peter Sagegun was not in his car when the police searched it. Saying that returning evidence to a crime scene should be overlooked in the name of justice simply doesn't work with me. Just a bad idea."

"I can't comment upon the ice pick."

"You shouldn't. Let's leave this history behind us."

"The discovery of the ice pick in the rocker panel of the car lead to the crime being solved. When it comes to winter rules of golf in July, you are not so ethical."

"If we both play the same rules, my ethics are not in question. Besides we don't have money on out games."

Abel shrugged, handed him a thumb drive, and a signed declaration stating that he saw Dalton on the day Silas was attacked in the park.

"I thought you would want a statement from me. The thumb drive contains the statement I am giving you, the video of Dalton hitting Levi, and the one from the park as well."

"Are you sure the color of the shirts is identical?"

"I saw Dalton was in his car. I saw the top of the shirt. He sits tall in his BMW. "

"My friend, lunch is on me." Laconia beamed

"It's your turn to buy."

"Let's not spoil the moment with accounting principles," grinned Laconia.

17

When Benis Dalton, his wife Sheri, and their two small children moved next door, Jeff McDonald was pleased. Dalton was a realtor, and his wife was a Deputy Sheriff in a neighboring county. He thought it was great to have a professional family in the neighborhood. Dalton's father had visited them from New York, and he thanked Jeff for welcoming his son into the neighborhood. As the father was leaving, he said, "I hope it works out this time." At that time Jeff hadn't thought about what the older man was telling him, but now he understood. Within a year of Dalton moving next door, Jeff put his home up for sale and began looking for a new home in a new city. Such was his hatred and fear of Dalton and his doubt that the police would ever protect him from Dalton.

He previously noticed Dalton playing with his kids in their backyard which was next to McDonald's backyard. Dalton and the boys roamed from their backyard into his where he had a vegetable garden. He saw the wife in the backyard and called to her. He explained the situation and hoped she would do something about it. He complimented her on always looking good. She even wore makeup whenever she stepped outside. She seemed nice, and he noticed that she always wore long sleeve shirts or sweatshirts. He asked her why. She said that she sunburned easily. He said that he was surprised that with her skin color she would be afraid of burning. She said that she didn't like her skin to turn dark, but that it didn't burn. Then she stopped the conversation by saying she had things to do inside.

The running through his garden happened several times, and when he saw Dalton, he mentioned that he preferred they not use his yard. Dalton protested that it was an open area, and there was no fixed boundary. He even questioned whether the back area was really owned by McDonald and not the house facing the street behind them. The conversation ended with Dalton asking if he had complained about any white kids playing in the back area. McDonald assured him that until they used the back area, it was never an issue.

A week later, all of the tomato plants in his garden were uprooted and all his vegetables trampled. He installed a surveillance camera.

The neighbor on the other side of Dalton saw her rose bushes plowed over with a front loader. When she confronted Dalton, he said that he thought the roses were on his property. He then ended the conversation by chest bumping her. McDonald saw what happened and ran to her side. Dalton stomped away, saying that he knew his rights, and they were harassing him. McDonald called after him, saying that all they wanted was peace and quiet. A few days later, Dalton installed a loudspeaker and began shouting the Sunni Call to Prayer, "I bear witness that there is no god but God alone, with no partner, and Muhammad is His servant and Messenger, and the Lord God's chosen messenger is Muhammad, and Islam is His religion." When McDonald asked him why he was doing that, Dalton said he was a Muslim, and it was his religious right to call the Muslims' prayer. He added that if infidels didn't like it, that was just too bad. McDonald installed double paned windows in his house, and Dalton began broadcasting over the loudspeaker the speeches of Louis Farrakhan and Mendelssohn Concertos. When McDonald complained about the violin concertos not being very religious, Dalton said that Farrakhan was the leader of the Nation of Islam, and everything he did was religious. He further said that

Farrakhan's followers had every right to play his music night and day.

When McDonald saw Dalton at a grocery store, he asked Dalton when he would stop his childish retaliations because all he wanted was peace and quiet. In response, Dalton jabbed a finger into his chest. McDonald then pushed Dalton back, causing a rack of comic books to crash to the floor. Dalton punched a jab into McDonald's jaw and walked away. The manager called the police, and the beat cop took down their statements. He also took the store's security tape into custody. Weeks later, McDonald learned that the tape was lost, and there was no record of the incident on file with the police.

On the day that McDonald learned the videotape that would have proved he was assaulted had disappeared, he hired a surveyor to mark out the boundaries of his property. A few days after the stakes were marked out, Dalton received a certified copy of the report that said McDonald was hiring a crew to install a six-foot high chain-link fence to run the length of his property abutting Dalton's property.

As the post diggers and bags of quick drying cement were unloaded, Dalton rushed out of his house with a pickax raised above his head while demanding that they stop.

"You are on my property!" he shouted. "You will damage my sprinklers! "Get out!"

"I had it surveyed!" yelled back McDonald, directing the work crew to move away from him. They retreated to the side of the house, and he called the police to report that a man with a pickax was threatening him.

They never came when he previously complained about late night noises, but this time they came quickly in two squad cars. He recognized one of the police officers from the grocery store altercation.

As the third squad car arrived, Sheri Dalton raced out of their front door with the youngest child on her hip and her police badge raised. "I'm a cop!" she shouted. "I'm a cop!"

She and the three police officers conferred in private, then Dalton said he had to go to work and dropped the pickax by the side of his house. Sheri and the child went back inside her house with one of the police officers. The police questioned McDonald for over three hours about the fence and why he wanted it. "Aren't you really making things worse by installing a fence?" said one cop. McDonald was questioned several times about the need for a fence. "Do you have a permit for the fence?" the police asked a number of times. Equally as many times, McDonald repeated, "Because the fence is less than seven feet high and made of chain-links, a permit is not needed." He continued, "Why aren't you questioning Dalton about the pickax? He threatened us." "We will get to that," said the lead officer who had been questioning Sheri inside her house. "We can't stand guard over your project," he warned. McDonald replied, "I have security cameras, and they will record if the fence posts are disturbed." The police continued, "You need to make the Daltons feel welcome in the neighborhood." "We were welcoming until Dalton went crazy," McDonald retorted. "They tell a different story," insisted the officer. "This fence doesn't seem like the act of a friendly neighbor," said a second officer. "I am building my fence," said McDonald. Another officer said, "Sir, it sounds like you are not a very friendly neighbor."

"People need to learn how to be good neighbors," said an officer.

"I am building my fence!" exclaimed McDonald. "And if I must, I will run a conduit to the fence and electrify it. That is my good neighbor policy. Tell him that! Just leave me alone!"

"If you take the law into your own hands, we will put your hands into handcuffs," said the second officer.

"He is the one you should tell about obeying the law. Tell him I have security cameras on the fence line. He better not mess with the posts."

On the first day, all the posts were installed along the fence line at ten-foot intervals. Three days later after the cement had set, the crew came back and hooked up the chain-link fence. As the crew pulled away, Laconia and McCoy pulled up in front of the Dalton house. Sheri answered the door. Laconia and McCoy introduced themselves and asked to speak with Benis.

"I'm a Deputy Sheriff. What is this about?"

"It's about us wanting to speak to your husband," said McCoy.

"I have a right to know."

"So does he, and we will tell him," said Laconia with a smile that invited compliance.

She showed them into a far room that was lined with books. Some of them were about how to be a better salesman. Most of the books were by Louis Farrakhan. Also on the bookshelf were videos of his speeches and CDs of his musical recitals. On the walls were various family photos, and a picture of a younger Benis wearing white boxing trunks, headgear, and the oversized gloves of Golden Glove competitors.

"What weight did you compete in?" asked Laconia.

"125," smiled Benis. "But I gave it up. Much too hard on my hands."

"That can happen," said McCoy.

"Why are you here?" asked Sheri.

"My name is Sergeant Laconia Jones."

"I'm Detective Steve McCoy," said McCoy.

"I thought this was all over. If McDonald wants a fence, he can have it. I was just upset when I saw them putting it up." Laconia and McCoy nodded as if they understood, and Dalton raced on. "It's a shame that he feels threatened by a Black family living next door to him. We have tried to be good neighbors, but all he could do was complain about my kids touching his grass and then accusing me of pulling up his tomato plants. When I saw the chain-link fencing truck, all I could think about was Mandela imprisoned on an island for twenty-seven years. It was like he wanted to imprison me and put my kids, my wife, and me in a small box. I have a right to live here. I am a professional; I sell real estate. Sheri is a Deputy Sheriff up north. From the beginning, all our gestures of goodwill have been met with suspicion and cold shoulders."

"We're sorry to hear that," said McCoy.

Ignoring McCoy, Dalton focused his eyes on Laconia. "You must know what it's like to be treated differently. No one uses the N-word anymore, but they still treat us with suspicion. At the corner grocery store when the clerk gives me change, he is careful to not let his fingers touch my palm. That has happened to you, hasn't it?"

"We're not here about your neighbor or his fence," said Laconia.

"Why did you let me talk on and on about the fence?" demanded Dalton.

"You just started talking."

"And you don't know how to interrupt a person?" snapped Sheri. "Then why are you here?"

"We are here about an incident in the People's Park three months ago."

"Three months ago?" gasped Dalton. "You expect me to remember something about the People's Park from three months ago?"

"You have been at the Peoples' Park, haven't you?"

"I sometimes take my lunch there. My wife makes a great egg salad sandwich, and I like to sit on one of the benches from time to time. Did someone claim that I didn't pick up my brown bag? I admit it. That happens sometimes. I get to thinking about a million-dollar sale I might close, and my mind wanders. I am a very successful real estate agent."

"We have an eye witness that places you there and a video."

"I just said I go there from time to time."

"Do you normally get into fights when you're eating an egg salad sandwich?" asked Laconia.

"No, not normally," sneered Dalton.

"I read about the incident at the YMCA. You were in a fight there. You said that you were eating an egg salad sandwich sitting in your car when your car got dinged."

"That had nothing to do with the egg salad sandwich. I simply wanted the officers to understand that I was only in my car minding my own business when this cracker slammed his car door into my car. I was in a BMW, and he treated it like the trashy vehicle he was driving – an old white van. The other guy was charged with assaulting me. For reasons I don't understand, the case was dismissed. He assaulted me and left marks on my face."

"The officers who went to the YMCA said that you claimed to have marks, but they didn't see any," replied Laconia.

"Those were white cops, and as you must know, marks show up differently on us colored folk. You must know that?"

"You don't have to talk to them, honey," said Sheri.

"Am I under arrest?"

"No, we are just gathering information," said Laconia. "If you don't want to talk to us, you don't have to. We are investigating a crime, and we merely want to know what you know."

"What is the crime?"

"The man you had a fight with died."

"How do you know I fought with him?"

"We are not at liberty to say right now. If you are charged, then the discovery file will be made available to you. If you have information that might cause us to not have you charged, now would be a good time to tell us. But you are under no obligation to talk to us."

"Hard to sell houses if you're in jail on a murder charge," said McCoy.

"I suspect so," said Laconia.

"Was the fellow who died an older gentleman who dresses in colorful suits?"

"Yes," said Laconia.

"I was eating my egg salad sandwich just watching the people in the park. I am a people watcher. Two boys were playing on a swing set, and an older woman came over and started talking to me. She was the grandmother or a friend of their mother. I forget which."

"Did you get her name?"

Dalton paused and looked up at the ceiling as if searching for the name, and then shook his head. "No. No idea who she was."

"As you were saying," said Laconia, taking a notebook out of his sports coat's inner pocket. "I want to make sure I remember accurately what you tell us."

Both Laconia and McCoy had small notebooks, and as Dalton spoke, they took notes.

"There is not a lot to say. The old woman and I were talking, and the older man came over cussing and shouting at the woman, then at me. It's disgusting, but I think he thought she was trying to pander the boys to me for immoral purposes."

"Why would he think that?" asked McCoy.

"No idea. But the older man became violent, poked a finger into my chest, and called me a pervert. He was shouting, and I pushed him away."

"You didn't hit him?"

"No, my hands are almost lethal weapons," Dalton said, pointing to the boxing photograph. "I know how to defend myself, but I would never hit an old man."

"He did fall down on the ground. We have witnesses," said Laconia.

"He stumbled backwards, but I caught him before he hit the ground and gently guided him to the ground," said Dalton. "That is what happened. It was such a minor event I forgot about it."

"The witnesses said you hit him."

"They were mistaken. I remember two young women in tight jeans with large earrings. They were far away and came over. The shouting must have alerted them to something going on. They must have had a bad angle to see what really happened. If they say I hit him they are mistaken. I am a professional, and my wife is a Deputy Sheriff. I would never hit an old man."

"You don't remember the name of the older woman or the names of the two boys?" asked Laconia.

"No, I do not," Dalton answered.

"I think you have taken up enough of our time," said Sheri.

"Thank you for your time," said Laconia.

From their front window, Dalton and Sheri watched the two police officers drive away. Turning to his wife, Dalton said, "I need you to get me the address of Linda Garvey."

18

Randy Jarad lay awake much of the night enjoying the warmth of Linda Garvey's big bed and wondering why so much of what pleased Mama Garvey made him uncomfortable. He wanted to please her, but the more he pleased her, the more he felt like he was falling into a deep cave he could not explain. He had touched a boy at gym class, and the boy screamed at him and ran away. When the teacher asked what he had done, he only began to cry and say it was an accident. A terrible accident. The teacher told him that it was okay, and accidents happen. But from then on, the other boys stayed away from him. Mama Garvey said he was a good boy and not to care what they thought. Because he was with Mr. Jones the evening before, Mama Garvey let him sleep in her bed, under the covers where it was warm and safe. He slipped out of bed quietly so as not to disturb Mama Garvey or his brother who was on the far side almost smothered in the large rolls of her flesh. He went to the kitchen and fixed himself a bowl of Cheerios and ate facing the wall in the living room.

"You can eat at the table," Garvey said, messing his hair up with her meaty hands. "Mr. Jones likes you. He is pleased with you. You can eat at the table this morning."

"Thank you, Mama Garvey," he said, reaching up to her hand and letting her pull him up to his feet.

"I love you, Randy," she said. "I love you and Baily. It would hurt me a lot if you were taken away from me."

"We are staying with you," said Randy. "Don't make us go away."

"I want you to stay, but them judges want to break us up. You don't want to live with your grandma, do you? She's mean, isn't she?"

"I want to stay with you," said Randy.

"Remember when your mom used to beat you? You remember that, don't you?"

"I suppose so," he said.

"I stopped her from hitting you. It was your grandma who taught her to hit children. I don't blame you for not remembering that. It was so painful to see that I won't forget it as well. You put that in the back of your mind, and lock it away."

Randy nodded as if he understood because it certainly was true that he didn't remember being beaten. So it must be as she said. It must be true, and he had forgotten the beatings because they were so bad.

"You can make yourself some toast, and make some for your brother."

"Can we have cinnamon toast?" he asked.

"Yes," she said. "Now the two of you should be quiet; I have to read some."

In a large envelope was a letter from Blount and the records of the Korean Women's Association. In the letter Blount complained about the amount of time he was devoting to her case, and he expected Abel to argue that the records of the association showed she was not in good health and unable to care for the children. She was in a bind, and she did not like that. If she suddenly announced to the Korean Women's Association that her health was better, she might not qualify for a daily caregiver. Once she was rid of Lori Black, she could get back to skimming off some of her caregiver's pay. She was certain that the next one would be easy to intimidate. The ones before all had been. So far Lori Black resisted her demand for a kickback. But at least she did not balk at doing chores for the boys, such as taking them to school and helping them with school projects.

Blount had promised her that neither Denise or Roberta would get custody of the boys, and it was just a matter of going through the motions, but that lawyer Abel did seem to understand that his efforts would fail. Randy and Baily had Cowlitz convinced that they were afraid of their mother and grandmother. They had even convinced her that they were afraid of a cousin who Randy said tried to kiss him. She had asked Blount, "How long must I be under a microscope?" In response, Blount only shrugged and said that a favorable report from the Parenting Investigator should resolve the issue. However, so far nothing had been resolved, and every two weeks the boys spent more time out of the house away from her. They were spending every other weekend in their grandmother's care. Blount could not say how long that would go on. "I would think that them saying they're afraid of their grandmother would be enough," she said to Blount. But he said the court needed more information to stop the visits. What that was he wouldn't say.

She tossed the papers aside in disgust. What was the point of having a counselor and a lawyer if she couldn't get what she wanted? She was brooding on the unfairness of life. She had worked long and hard to get the welfare that she was receiving, and she did not want to lose any of it.

She had Randy brew up some coffee and bring her a cup, with creamer and three sugars. The boy knew what pleased her. It would be a shame to lose him. Not only did she collect welfare for him, but Jones – or whatever his real name was – paid well for his time with the boy. She wondered if she could get Rand to accuse his mother, Denise, of abuse during one of the counseling sessions whether it would be enough to stop the visits with the mother and grandmother. The danger, of course, was that the counselor might report the abuse to Child Protective Services. Then they might investigate not only the Jarads but her as well. It was complicated and required consideration of all the possibilities down the line. She was peering into the future as best she could when Lori Black arrived.

"Ready for your insulin?" Lori asked.

"Not now," Garvey replied. "Robert Culpepper, the court investigator, is coming over in two hours. I need you to clean the house extra careful. He was a Marine and likes things tidy. He told me that he can tell when a person is lying to him. I love it when a man tells me that he can't be fooled. Those are the biggest fools of all," she cackled. "I need to look exhausted as if I just cleaned the place up. Hurry and clear out of here until I call you." She waved her cell phone back and forth. "Then you can come back and give me the shot. While you are gone you can run some errands for me."

"What kind of errands?"

"Shopping. Here's a list," she said, and handed her a sheet of paper. "Has anyone called you to ask about me?"

"No, why?"

She held up the large envelope with the records from the Korean Women's Association and slammed it on the floor. "I asked you a question, and when I ask a question I expect an answer, not a question. Again, Lori, has anyone called and asked about what you do for me?"

"No."

"John Abel has not called and asked you what you do for me?"

"No, who is that?" Lori asked. She flinched at what she expected would be a torrent of rebuke.

"He is Denise and Roberta's lawyer. You must tell me if he does, and you must tell him nothing. I forbid you to tell him anything. I have a right to my privacy, and you are to tell him nothing. Just like a doctor or a priest can't blab about what a person says. Do you understand?"

"I understand."

"Get the place cleaned up, and dust under the tables. He is a Marine. He may march around here wearing white gloves for all I know. If he finds anything wrong I will get you fired. I will say you stole from me, and you'll never work for the association ever again!"

Lori hurried through her morning chores of vacuuming, cleaning the toilets, cleaning up the kitchen, making the beds, and dusting. She also checked that the boys brushed their teeth, washed their faces, and were wearing clean clothes. After Lori left, Garvey instructed the boys on what they were to say and not say to the man who was coming to visit them. "Remember, I will hear everything you say! So, you'd better tell him what I told you to say, or you and I might end up homeless on the street."

"Yes, Mama Garvey," they both said, nodding their heads in unison.

When the court investigator arrived, they were in their bedroom. Baily was working on a coloring book of farm animals, and Randy was reading a story out of *Boy's Life*. The story was about a boy who trained to beat a rich bully in a swimming contest. He won a lot of new friends by doing so, including the girl next door. He had been sweet on her for years, yet too shy to speak to her. It was a great story, and he had read it several times.

The court investigator, Robert Culpepper, was in his mid-sixties. He had close cropped, light brown hair. He wore a sports coat over a polo shirt and tan Dockers. He knocked on the front door at 10 a.m., the exact time he had told her was his ETA. "Your what?" she had asked. "My estimated time of arrival," he explained, and she thanked him for helping her with her confusion. She explained that she was a simple person who hadn't traveled much.

"Would you like to see the boys' room?" Garvey asked when the investigator first entered.

"Of course," he said.

The boys were on their beds that were neatly made. Their toys were neatly arranged on a bookshelf. They smiled at him, and he smiled back.

"Hello," the boys said in unison.

"How are you boys today?"

"We're fine," said Randy.

"Mama Garvey takes good care of us," volunteered Baily.

"Would you like to talk to them more?" Garvey interjected.

"Later," Culpepper said. "Could you please show me the rest of the house?"

"Of course," she meekly replied. She showed him throughout the house, and kept apologizing over and over again for how untidy things were. "I did a little tidying up, but I do my deep cleaning on Fridays," she explained.

"It all looks good to me," he said. He opened the refrigerator and noticed the open jars of sauce, with the dates on top of them indicating when they were opened.

"I like to be sure that everything is fresh, and nothing is wasted," Garvey explained.

"Very nice," murmured Culpepper, making a notation in a notebook. "Perhaps we could talk in the living room."

"Would you like the boys to join us?"

"No," said Culpepper. "On second thought, let's talk in the kitchen since it's farther away from the boys' room."

"Of course. I made some coffee. Would you like a cup?"

"That would be nice. Black."

He sat silently as Garvey bustled about getting coffee and setting out a tray of assorted cookies.

"I really shouldn't," said Culpepper, reaching for a chocolate chip cookie. He reached for one and took a bite. "Delicious."

"I bake them myself."

"My wife would love to have the recipe."

"So, what would you like to know? The boys are happy here, and I would hate to see them uprooted from the routine they love. Denise has it all wrong. I didn't stop her from moving in or seeing the boys. She just wasn't interested in being their mom. I feel sorry for her. I suspect her mother, Roberta, put her up to wanting them back."

"I have read the reports from the counselor that your attorney sent me. They would be very afraid of being separated from you if they were forced to live with either their mother or grandmother."

"They are happy," said Garvey. "I haven't coached them at all."

"I'm sure that is true, but the children have seen another counselor, and she has concerns."

"What other counselor?"

"One that their grandmother has been taking them to during her weekends with the boys."

"Is that legal? I never authorized that. Does my attorney know?"

"No, he only recently learned about it in a letter from Abel."

"I have not seen it."

"I am sure you will get a copy."

"But can they do that? Just take the boys to a counselor without me knowing about it?"

"It is unusual and unorthodox, but there was no order entered with the court prohibiting it."

"So, Abel allowed the children to go to another counselor behind my back? Did the boys know they were seeing a counselor? They said nothing to me."

"It was sly the way they did it. The counselor simply asked them a few questions each time they saw her, and never said she was a therapist. She's suggested that the boys are being coached by you to act up whenever they are with their mother or grandmother."

"That is absurd!" gasped Garvey, clutching her breast with indignation.

"You have a right to know about these accusations. Now, it is important that you say nothing to the boys."

"Of course not," said Garvey. "Their little lives have gone through enough torment to be placed in the middle of a child custody case. I won't say a word."

"Good," said Culpepper. "The boys are doing well in school. It is important that they have stability and not have their lives disrupted by legal proceedings."

"I could not agree more," smiled Garvey, pushing the plate of cookies toward Culpepper.

Culpepper noticed that Garvey was starting to sweat profusely. Her lack of insulin was taking its toll on her. "Are you all right?" he asked.

"I am fine. I just worry so much about these little dears of mine. I never had children, but they are as close to me as if they were my own. I just hate—" she paused for a moment and took a sip of water. "I just hate the thought of them going back to their mother. I think she drove her husband to suicide, and I fear what may be in store for them once all the court proceedings are over."

"It is my job to look out for their best interests," said Culpepper. "And from what I can see, it is in their best interests that you remain the primary custodian. Are you concerned about them seeing their mother and grandmother?"

"No, no," said Garvey. "Children need to know their blood. But I think their visits should be regulated with the understanding that they stay with me where they are the happiest."

"I am glad to hear that you don't want to shut out their mother and grandmother. I was afraid of that. They seem to think that is what the boys want."

"Not at all. It's me they want to cut out of the children's lives. Me, who stepped up and cared for them when neither of those women did. No, I would not deprive the mother and grandmother of staying in their life, but they need to understand that they're not in charge."

"What does that mean?"

"It simply means we prepared a parenting plan and visitation schedule that sets out their boundaries. They can come to school events and see the kids, but on a regular schedule. The boys need a regular schedule."

"So true," said Culpepper. "Now, I will talk to the boys for a while."

His interview of the boys took less than a half hour in which he confirmed that they liked sports and seldom watched cartoons. When asked how they were disciplined, they each said that they are never spanked, and they are disciplined with short time-outs. They said that their time-outs are just what they need to mend their ways, as Mama Garvey often says.

Before Culpepper left, Garvey gave him the recipe for her chocolate chip cookies. "The secret is a pinch more of vanilla," she said. That was exactly what Lori said whenever she was asked what made the cookies so good.

Culpepper was driving away when Garvey called Blount to give him a piece of her mind. She told him what a coward he was. She went on a rampage over the phone, telling him that the skinny receptionist with no tits and a nasal drip as big as Niagara Falls should not run interference for him. That was prompted because on her first call the receptionist said he was with a client. On her second call, she said he was on the phone, and on her third call, she told Garvey that Blount was gone for the day. Garvey was so angry that she even made Baily sit next to his brother for an hour with his nose an inch from the wall. "What did I do?" wailed the little boy. "You didn't tell me all that went on at the devil grandmother's house!" she yelled. "Neither of you appreciate everything that I have done for you!" She demanded, "Now, be quiet or there will be no supper, no cartoons, and no warm bed for either of you!" She continued her tirade until Lori came back. Garvey gave the boys one final warning about following her orders. Randy and Baily simply sat still, ashamed of all they had done to make Mama Garvey angry with them.

Not long after the boys went to bed, with Randy in his room and Baily in Garvey's bed, there was a knock on the front door. Garvey looked out the window and saw that a black BMW was parked in front of the steps leading to her front door.

"Remember me?" smirked Dalton.

"You're the man who likes to eat lunch and watch little boys play in the park. You're the man who beat up Silas Smith the day before he died. I have not seen you for a while, but I remember who you are."

"You have it wrong. I didn't touch that man."

"Hmm. Hmm," Garvey said, while blocking the doorway.

"May I come in?" Dalton asked.

She showed him to the kitchen. A few chocolate chip cookies were left on the table. "Want some?" she asked.

"No, no. I want to talk to you about what you remember of the day in the park. Did the police come and talk to you?"

"Should they?"

"No, no, they shouldn't but they might. I want to know what you will say to them if they do show up."

"They must know that you had a fight with Silas, and you think they will find me?"

"I didn't touch that man. He accused me … well you know what he accused me of."

"I saw what I saw. You did more than touch him. Far more."

"I pulled my punches. I only wanted to scare him. I wouldn't hit an old man."

"You beat him to the ground; that's what I remember."

"Perhaps we could come to an understanding," said Dalton. "You rent this place, right? You get this house at a reduced rent because you claim Section 8 benefits."

"I may be poor, but I have my pride and integrity."

"Don't we all? But perhaps I could help you, and you could help me."

"You are good with your fists. I will give you that."

"I am not asking you to lie, just not to remember as well as you might."

181

Garvey smiled and pushed the cookie plate toward him. "Take one. I think friends should share a little food. Do you want me to be your friend?"

"Yes," Dalton answered.

"I have need of a man like you, all fit and strong."

Dalton almost choked on his cookie and coughed up a crumb. "What do you mean?" he gasped.

"I'll get you a glass of water. That BMW must have cost you a lot. You don't see them here in Center Point often."

"I am a real estate agent. I need to look good, but I don't have a lot of cash."

"$50,000 cash is what I need, and I'll need it before the police ask me any questions."

"How will I know that you won't ask for more?"

"Once I give the police a statement, I can't go back on my word without looking like a perjurer."

Dalton nodded, "I can give you $10,000."

"Do I look like I'm in a mood to barter? I ought to ask for more just for the insult. If I charged you $10,000 for every year you'd do in prison for the murder of Silas Smith, you would owe me over $200,000. Plus, no one will offer you better tasting cookies such as I am," she said, taking a giant bite out of a cookie.

"I will need some time to get you that much money."

"And there's one more thing you must do for me."

"What is that?"

"That is where your boxing skills come in," chuckled Garvey. "If you do what I want, I might even knock $10,000 off my asking price."

19

Randy went to the wall as directed by a stare and sharp jab in the air of Garvey's forefinger. Staring at the wall his mind would drift. Images would float into his mind and push other images out like clouds in the sky. Nothing would stay the same. His mother had told him that when he had unpleasant thoughts that he should put them in an imaginary jar and pretend they were trapped inside like a genie in a lamp that could do him no harm.

He had told the man with a strawberry patch of skin that he did not want to go get a happy meal. The man had smiled and said they were going to a mansion with lots of colorful fish that he could count and try to catch with his hands. What kind of fish are these, he had asked? The man had said they were Joy fish, at least that is what he thought the man had said. The woman who met him at the door had a doll face, smooth. Her lips hardly moved when she spoke.

She took them the back yard where there was a pond with many colored fish - white, black, red, orange, yellow, blue, brown and cream. Catch one, if you can, they said and he tried and tried. He waded into the water scooping up hand fulls of water, but no fish. He slipped and came up gasping and crying."Come here," the woman said, "and take off your clothes." "No, no!" he said, but they insisted and gave him a towel to wrap himself in. It was warm, blue and thick. Much thicker than the ones Mama Garvey had and not scratchy. The woman took his clothes to dry them and returned with a book of photographs. They were of a naked boy younger than him. The boy was peeing and laughing. "Do you like licorice?" The man asked. He said yes and they gave him a glass of ice and poured some

183

clear liquid from a bottle over the cubes. They poured some into their coffee cups. It was sweet. He smiled at them and they smiled at him. Later, she asked to take his photograph. He said, "Yes." She had him walk around the pond pointing at the fish. "Just walk," she said. As he walked she followed him, clicking her tongue. He had the towel wrapped about him but at her urging, he dropped it. He was dizzy. "Pee in the pond, the fish won't mind. They do it all the time. Pee like the Belgium boy," she said. The man with the strawberry patch clapped his hands. He wanted to make them happy. He was happy to be with them and hoped he would never return home, but he did. He was at the wall and suddenly he began to cry and he did not know why. He could not remember all that happened that day and he was not sure if he wanted to remember. He stared at the wall looking for answers for he felt so alone and had done something wrong, when all he had wanted to do was please the people he trusted. He had no answers for how ashamed he felt and the silly jar his mother had told him to put his troubles in was of no help at all. He knew if he cried, Mama Garvey would hit him and so he fought back the tears and waited to be told that he could move away from the wall that somehow he was afraid to leave.

Garvey heard the knock at the door and peeked out through a blind to see who it was. It was two men, one Black, one white. The Black man had broad shoulders, and his arms filled out the sleeves of his sports jacket. The white guy was taller and thinner, but his arms filled out the sleeves of his jacket as well. If it were social workers doing a home inspection, one of them would have been a woman. She wondered if the ER doctor who accused her of being a drug addict had filed a police report. She called out that she needed a moment and breathed a sigh of relief that they did not take that as a cue to bust down her door. She pulled Randy away from the wall and told him to watch cartoons with his brother. She did a quick check of the bathroom and her bedroom to see if she had any residue of crushed oxycodone lying around. She found none, straightened her unmade bed, and glanced in the mirror, smoothing a few loose strands of hair away from her forehead. Perhaps they were at her door because of Silas Smith, but she thought it best not to let them know what she suspected. She opened the door part way and asked who they were.

"I'm Detective Jones and this is Detective McCoy," said the Black man.

"I just fired the girl yesterday. I told the association that I wanted a new girl to help me out. I am disabled and care for two young children," she said. Before Laconia could speak, she rushed on. "Some money was missing from my handbag. I told Lori all she needed to do was to confess, and I'd forgive her, but she won't. That's why I called the association. I simply need a reliable honest helper. Is that too much to ask? I told them that I didn't want to press charges."

"We aren't here about a petty thief," blurted out McCoy.

"Perhaps a little missing money is of no concern to you, but I can tell you that a few dollars is a lot to me. I don't know how much she took, but I don't have much and anything gone is a great loss for me. I have two small children that I take care of, and I can barely make ends meet as it is."

"He didn't mean it that way," said Laconia. "We are here about an altercation you might have witnessed in the People's Park a few months ago."

"I don't want that poor girl to get into any more trouble on my account. If she was so poor that she needed to steal from me, she must have really needed the money. The Lord will judge her, not me."

"May we come in?" asked Laconia. "This won't take long."

She opened the door and directed them into the kitchen, whispering that she didn't want to disturb the boys who were watching cartoons. "It is a little treat I give them from time to time, and I don't want them hearing what we are talking about." she explained. As they sat down at the kitchen table, she offered them coffee or water which they declined.

McCoy took out a notebook and pen and waited for Laconia to begin.

"Do you know, or did you know Silas Smith?" asked Laconia.

"Of course, I know Silas. We were friends. I've known him since I was a child. Is this about his death?"

"Do you recall if Mr. Smith was in a fight with another man?"

"I wouldn't call it a fight but, yes, I recall him having loud words with another man. I don't know who the man was."

"You don't recall Mr. Smith being on the ground?"

Garvey stared off into space for a moment. "Yes, I do recall that. But, I'm not sure how he landed on the ground."

"What do you recall of the man Mr. Silas was having loud words with?"

"Fairly tall and athletically built. He was wearing a pink shirt and gray slacks. He looked professional. I never got his name. The incident was over in an instant."

"What else do you recall?"

186

"The boys were playing on the Big Toy. They were sliding up and down burning off some energy. The man had a brown bag, and he was sitting at the picnic table eating when Silas came over yelling at him."

"Where were you?"

"I was seated at the same picnic table, but the man and I had not spoken to one another. Silas came over and was angry. He accused the man of liking little boys, if you know what I mean."

"I know what you mean."

"Silas was adamant that the man had to leave the park and not come back. His voice was loud, and he began poking his finger into the man's chest. The man pushed him away, and Silas fell."

"Did you see the man strike Silas in the head or anywhere on his body?"

"No, no. Nothing like that. The man was much younger than Silas and did throw some punches toward his face. But each time he pulled up his punch. He didn't strike Silas."

"You are sure of that?" asked Laconia.

"Absolutely. After the man left, Silas and I talked for a while. I invited him over for dinner, and he came to my house that night. He looked fine, and we had a nice meal."

While they were talking, Randy came into the kitchen and asked if he could have a drink of water. "Of course, sweetie," Garvey said. She introduced the boys to Laconia and McCoy. She used the introduction as an opportunity to say how important it was to cooperate with the police and always tell the truth.

"Did Mr. Smith eat well?"

"Oh, yes, he didn't complain of any headache, or any other aches or pains. He even had second helpings. The man in the park didn't hurt him. Of that I'm certain."

"Thank you," said Laconia. "Would you mind if Detective McCoy writes in statement form what you've told us? Then, if it's correct, would you sign the statement?"

"I would be glad to. I thought somebody was already in jail for killing poor Silas."

"We are just tying up some loose ends," said Laconia.

As they were leaving, Garvey asked, "How did you find me?"

"It seems you are well known in the neighborhood. One clerk knew who you were when we mentioned that you had two small boys with you. He said that when you come into the store, he goes out of his way to keep an eye on you."

"Did he say why?"

"He just said that you were well known to many," Laconia replied. "He said that a woman who wears a heavy coat in the summertime is one to remember."

"Several other clerks said the same thing," added McCoy.

"I am an honest woman," Garvey emphatically said. "I get cold easily."

<u>20</u>

When Abel arrived at his office, he found a Temporary Restraining Order on the floor in front of his front door. It prohibited any further evaluations or consultations with a counselor or psychologist when the children were with Roberta or Denise Jarad until further order of the court. The order was signed by Commissioner Edmond Goldman and entered without giving notice to Abel. A hearing was set for two weeks out. The children were specifically allowed to continue therapy with counselor Debra Cowlitz. She was directed to file a report on what, if any, damage may have been done to the children and whether they'd been exposed to any questions by either Denise, Roberta, or another third party. At the end of the order it was stated that it had been entered to prevent harm to the children. In bold print was written:

VIOLATION OF THIS ORDER SHALL BE CONSIDERED CONTEMPT OF COURT AND SUBJECT THE VIOLATOR TO SANCTIONS, INCLUDING BUT NOT LIMITED TO INCARCERATION

Accompanying the order was a declaration signed by Garvey stating that the children had become progressively withdrawn after returning from visits with their mother and grandmother. It, also, stated that a "friend" of the grandmother was trying to convince them that they wanted to live with her. Additionally, it stated that after each visit, the boys said they did not want to go back to their grandmother. It further claimed that the grandmother was mean to them, she frowns when they ask to go home, and she tells them they are bad boys for not wanting to live with her.

Along with Garvey's declaration was a report from Culpepper. He began by stating that by statute, "The role of the guardian ad litem is to investigate and report factual information regarding the issues ordered to be reported or investigated to the court. The guardian ad litem shall always represent the best interests of the child." Culpepper's report continued, "I take this responsibility very seriously and always begin an investigation with no agenda other than finding out what is in the best interests of the child or children." *Bravo for sainthood*, thought Abel. In twenty years he had never experienced a lawyer condoning the taking of children to a professional without his knowledge and consent. However, he conceded that there was no order that prohibited taking the children to an unknown therapist. While taking the children to an unapproved therapist for evaluation was not in violation of a court order, he thought it improper. Blount suggested that while Abel was an experienced defense lawyer, he simply was unaware of the norms and protocols of family law. He was far less generous in asking for sanctions against Abel. He stated that the basis of his request was that Abel was underhanded and driving up the costs of the litigation. He went on to laud his own behavior as upholding the traditions of good practice, and he was defending Garvey without any remuneration other than the satisfaction of assisting a woman in need.

Culpepper expounded on his visit to the Garvey home as if he spent hours there. He found that the children were exceptionally well cared for, very polite, and happy. Culpepper said the house was immaculate, and he added that Garvey was an amazing baker. *A regular Mother Hubbard*, thought Abel.

Culpepper's opinion was that further sessions with the "grandmother's secret therapist" should be stopped immediately so as not to confuse the children.

Abel took a few deep breaths and decided to work on a response later. He knew sending the kids to a counselor to evaluate what was going on in the Garvey home was a risk, yet he also knew that he had little choice. With each report, the counselor Cowlitz seemed more resolved that the children should remain with Garvey. When he suggested that the children be interviewed by a specialist, he knew they might not find out anything. Instead, the specialist suspected that the children were terrified of Garvey. Abel thought Culpepper would at least want to know more, rather than shut down any opinions contrary to those he'd already formed. As Herbert Spencer said, "The surest path to ignorance is contempt prior to investigation." He found that quote at the back of the AA *Big Book*, and he cherished it. But he also knew that family law judges consider GALs the eyes and ears of the court. Some judges never disagreed with the recommendations of a guardian ad litem and preferred not to conduct trials. Abel knew the cliché, "A fool is as wise as his own conceit" is often the foundation of many court rulings.

There was no landline in Abel's office. All of his calls went to the business line at his home. Billie did not like going to the office, but as a concession, she agreed to field Abel's phone calls, and she passed them on to him. A text from her alerted him that a new client wanted to meet with him. He called the number she texted to him and introduced himself.

"I may be in some trouble and need advice," said the man. The voice seemed slightly muffled.

191

"What kind of trouble?"

"Criminal trouble. I was stopped for driving under the influence."

"Have charges been filed yet?"

"Not yet, but I would like to meet with you to discuss options."

"I could meet with you tomorrow morning. I usually meet potential clients during the morning."

"I work. If possible, I'd rather meet with you this evening after work. My friend, Levi Yabroff, says you are a good lawyer, and I'll pay for your time."

"You are a friend of Levi's?"

"We are very close."

"Okay, I can see you next Tuesday at 6. What is your name?"

"Benjamin Dawkins. I know where you are. I'll be there next Tuesday at 6 p.m.," the man said. Then he quickly disconnected the call.

The restraining order did not prevent the weekend visitations with Denise and Roberta, but it did prevent them from discussing the case with the two boys or the boys being interviewed by the counselor again. Abel had not revealed to Culpepper that he also had a professional supervisor go to the house while the boys were with his clients. She, too, was of the opinion that Garvey was encouraging the boys to act up and throw tantrums while they were with their mother and grandmother. He called the evaluator, and they discussed the need for her to be vigilant, and prepare a declaration of her observations the following week. The more Abel got to know Roberta, the more he believed that she only wanted what was best for her two grandchildren. Culpepper did not disagree with her good intentions, but he also thought Garvey wanted only the best for the two boys. However, when the mother sought help with raising the boys, she gave custody to Garvey, not to her mother, Roberta. Because Garvey reneged on her agreement to help Denise learn how to parent the boys, it gave them a basis for their argument, but Abel knew he needed more. He just wasn't sure what more he needed. He originally thought that Marsha Barnes' declaration would have been enough to alert Culpepper to Garvey's greed and manipulation of others. But he had accepted Blount and Garvey's explanation that Barnes was a disgruntled person with a drug problem who Garvey unsuccessfully tried to help withdraw from her addictions. Abel had tried to contact Barnes, but unfortunately she had disappeared.

Abel was reading the restraining order and the declarations that came with it for the fourth time when there was a knock on his front door. It was a soft knock that he barely heard. His office was a two-story house which was converted into an office before he bought it. It was not uncommon for people to knock on the door rather than just enter. "Hello," said a woman.

"I am coming. I should have a sign that says just enter. I am coming," Abel called out. He was wearing jeans and a chambray work shirt with the tail untucked to cover his cross draw holster. He made sure that the holster was covered and went to answer the door.

"I'd like to speak to the lawyer, Abel," said the woman.

"I am Abel."

"You are John Abel, the lawyer? You don't look like a lawyer."

"I am. I clean up well with a suit and tie when I have court. Who are you?"

"My name is Lori Black. I'm here about Linda Garvey. Do you know who she is?"

"All too well. Please come in," Abel said, opening the door wide for her.

Lori explained that she was the caregiver for Linda Garvey, and she had information that she wanted to share with him. Abel invited her in, and he pointed to a chair on the other side of the desk from where he was seated.

"How did you get my name?"

"Garvey leaves court papers lying around the house. I saw your name on the documents, and she mentions your name often. She doesn't like you," Lori said, sitting down.

"Why are you here? How can I help you? Did Garvey send you?"

"No, just the opposite," said Lori. "I want to help you."

"If you work for Garvey, why do you want to help me?"

"I want to help the boys. I have just seen too much. This morning Randy, the older boy, came into the house while I was cleaning. He had spent the night at a Mr. Jones' house. When the man came into the house, he glared at me and hustled Garvey into the other room. I heard them arguing. When the man came out of the back room, he rushed past me. I think he was trying to avoid me seeing him and being able to recognize him. I asked Randy if everything was okay, and he sighed and went to sit in front of the wall without being told to. It breaks my heart to see how she has beaten him down."

"In front of the wall?"

"That is one of the things Garvey makes the boys do when she is angry with them. Baily is her favorite. It is Randy who is the most disciplined. Baily might sit in front of the wall for a half hour. Randy sits there for hours. They do what they can to please her, and she is always telling them that she is upset with them. I want to help them. How can I help them?"

"You could tell me more, and I could prepare a declaration for you to sign."

"Can we do that now?"

"Of course," said Abel. "But if you give me a statement, you'll not be able to work for Garvey any longer."

"I don't care about that," said Lori. "I can't watch what she does to the boys any longer. If the Korean Women's Association can't find me another person to work for, then I will find work elsewhere."

For the next two hours Lori told Abel what she knew, after which he took her words and drafted a declaration for her to sign. He wanted to get her statement that day other than risk her having second thoughts about signing a declaration. But the more they talked, the more he realized that she would have no second thoughts. After she signed the declaration, they shook hands and she left. A few moments later she knocked again. She held a plastic bag in her hand.

"Please give this to Randy when you can."

"What is it?" asked Abel.

"It is a small wooden bat, the kind they give out at baseball parks. His dad gave it to him, and Garvey tossed it away. I retrieved it from the trash, and I want him to have it. Until now, though, I've felt that if he got it back, then Garvey would take it away again. It is still messy. I haven't cleaned it off."

"That's okay. Why did she toss it away?"

"I am not sure. I just know it's precious to Randy, and Garvey was adamant that it had to be thrown away. Randy was heartbroken to lose a gift from his dad. I retrieved it from the trash. I knew that if I gave it to him, she would just throw it away again. So, I put it in the trunk of my car and just remembered it. I've kept it in the trunk since the day I got it. Will you give it to him when he is safe and away from Garvey?"

"I will," said Abel. "You don't know more about why she wanted to throw it away?"

Lori shook her head that she did not. "The night before they had a guest for dinner. An important person. Garvey wanted the place cleaned. She said the boys' mother was cooking something special for an important guest. The boys were excited to spend some extra time with Denise. The next morning there were extra dishes in the sink for me to wash. Whoever it was, she wanted to impress him, even though she didn't like him. She referred to him as 'an old man.' She wondered what color of suit he would show up wearing, pink or yellow. She said the man was an embarrassment to the community. But he was also someone she wanted to impress. The bat was inside a plastic bag. I should clean it up."

"No, leave it as it is. You don't know why she wanted to get rid of it. So let's just leave it as it is for now," said Abel. The more he knew about Garvey, the less he believed anything she ever did was legal. "Is there anything else you haven't told me?"

"I haven't told you the whole truth. Can you forgive me?"

"I am a defense attorney, so I'm used to being lied to. What haven't you told me?"

She took a deep breath, swallowed, and cautiously continued, "She said if I didn't give her half my pay, she was going to report me as a thief. She's said that in the past, but this time I could tell it was her final warning. So I told her that I quit and left."

"Why didn't you tell me before?"

"I was afraid you would believe her and think that I was lying to protect myself."

"I believe you. The more I know about Garvey, the more I believe she's the reincarnation of a Dachau prison guard. We need to revise your declaration."

For another hour, Lori sat across from Abel, giving him additional information to include in her declaration on his computer. He'd read it to her, and she would confirm that what he wrote was accurate or not. Finally, the revised declaration was suitable for her signature, and he printed it for her.

"Thank you," she said as she was leaving. "Whether I work for the association ever again or not, I am glad that I finally told my story."

Fortified by the unexpected revelations of Lori Black, Abel began to draft a brief listing of the similarities between what Marsha Barnes previously told him and what Lori Black told him that afternoon. In addition, there were many contradictions regarding Garvey's applications for health care assistance and her claim that she was physically able to care for the two children. Plus, through the Korean Women's Association records, he obtained Garvey's medical records for numerous emergency room visits when, for one reason or another, she had attempted to get narcotics for pain management. On her last visit, the ER doctor who worked shifts at several hospitals recognized her from a visit the day before. Having already written a prescription for a ten-day supply of oxycodone, he simply couldn't understand why she was out of medication unless she was an addict or selling the pills. She left the hospital in a huff, accusing him of being a bigot and discriminating against her because of her weight and having no sympathy for the actual pain she suffered. Abel had caught her in so many lies, he didn't think it possible that he would lose in court. However, the arrogance and gullibility of judges should never be underestimated, nor, as he had to admit, the over confidence of an advocate.

21

The editor of the local bar news magazine liked Abel's editorial about the difficulty of detecting concealed anger and asked him to write another article. He readily agreed to do another article and realized he really did not have any topic in mind that he wanted to write about. He tried to think of a topic, but could not think of one. So, he went to a local coffee shop to drink an Americano, surf the internet and perhaps find an idea worth pursuing. The coffee shop was the Bluebeard Cafe. It roasted its own coffee in an area next to the espresso stand. It was in an old building that was once a car garage. The floor was cement, and it had large bay doors that were partially open in the summertime for a pleasant breeze. The patrons were mainly art students from a nearby university. At every table were laptops, books, or drawing pads. Most of the students had either tattoos or eye and nose piercings and sometimes both. Some of the patrons were older and appeared to be day laborers or retired. It was not a place for men in suits and ties. On the walls were posters for upcoming musical events headlined by grunge bands. The music was loud, the chatter insistent and for reasons he could not understand it was an excellent place for Abel to think of new ideas. The more he disregarded the racket around him the more ideas would sometimes float before him. Unoccupied tables were always in short supply. When he saw a empty table, he put his laptop and went to the stand to order an Americano. When he returned to the table he had laid claim to by setting his laptop on it, he found Rob Washington sitting at his table reading a local newspaper. He was not as scruffy as he remembered him but he remembered him well.

"Remember me?"

"I remember you very well. I may forget a face, or a name from time to time, but I never forget the name and face of a man who pulls a gun on me. I am funny that way. What do you want?"

"You aren't mad about that are you. I was under a lot of stress."

"I am sure you were. You shared some of it with me."

"I talk to Riley from time to time, and I visit him sometimes. It helps me to stay calm if I can help someone else."

"That is how it works," Abel said.

"He says you are helping him.

"I've given his lawyer a couple of suggestions that he has followed up on. Are you still homeless?"

"The wife may be dropping the divorce and giving me a second chance. Turns out Huffman is as bad a drunk as I am. He just hides it better than me, but he got suspended from his job for pointing a gun at Jeffery Adams, the homeless do-gooder. Turns out Adam's brother is a lawyer. He filed a complaint against Huffman."

"Occasionally justice prevails."

"I was screwed, representing myself. Judges favor people with lawyers."

"Some lawyers would say judges bend over backwards for people who represent themselves. Let them file papers late, don't enforce the rules of hearsay as strictly as they do against a lawyer and always make the lawyer responsible for drafting up the final papers."

"You know I'm right, don't you?"

Abel sighed and nodded. "If I tried to build a house it would leak. Everyone is better at something than others.

Overall, I think you are right. Why are you telling me this?"

"Because I want you to do something. Riley said you write articles. He told me about your magazine article. I looked it up and showed it to my wife. I told her that it was unfair of her to pass her hatred on to our kids."

"That helped you get back together?"

"Huffman getting suspended helped more, but yes, your article helped a little. So, write one about how people should not be looked down on because they don't have a lawyer. Can you do that?"

"I can try," said Abel.

"Riley says you are helping. How is it going?"

"We will see," said Abel.

"I am sorry about pointing the gun at you." Washington stuck out his hand. Abel took it. "You aren't a bad guy for a guy who wears a suit," said Washington and he walked away.

Before Abel had even had time to open his laptop, Benis Dalton sat down where Washington had been sitting. He was wearing a powder blueTommy Bahama sweatshirt with half zipper, blue jeans and the same shoes that Abel had seen the video of him attacking Silas Smith. Casual shoes with dark brown top and wide white sides. They were the kind of shoes that dressed down a suit and dressed up a pair of jeans. "This where you troll for clients, counselor?"

"I come for the peace and quiet," said Abel. Over the loudspeaker, Édith Piaf was belting out Non, je ne regrette rien"

"One of your clients pulled a gun on me, and I know you must be the one who got the police after me for the death of some preacher. What have you got against me? What did I ever do to you?"

"When David pulled a gun on you, he did you a favor. He stopped you from murder or a first degree assault charge. You are lucky he had the training and restraint not to just shoot you when he pulled out his gun. Just to be clear, he was not my client when he pulled the gun on you. He became my client afterwards. About the death of Silas Smith, that is on you. I have seen the video. Pity he didn't have a gun."

"I never hit him, I just scared him."

"Like I said I saw the video."

"You calling me a liar," Dalton shouted.

"Time for you to go," said one of the Bistros approaching the table with another behind him.

"Sure, take his side. You're taking his side because he is white. I know how this plays out."

"I am taking his side because you came to his table and he has never caused any trouble here before. You, I don't know."

"So people of my kind don't come here? Is that what you are saying?" shouted Dalton. "We were just talking and he insulted me. See if I come here again," he said and stalked off.

"What was that about?" asked the bistro.

"Not sure, but I think he wanted an excuse to hit me or for me to hit him, perhaps. Thanks for coming over."

"Everything ok?"

"This was the best Americano I have had in a long time," said Abel lifting up the cup. "I came in here with no ideas and now I have more than I know what to do with."

22

For reasons unknown to Abel, the Jarad case was deemed a
high conflict case by a court administrator, and all motions
were to be heard by the judge assigned to the case. That
judge was Marilyn Nightingale. She was a new judge
whose previous experience was defending employers and
manufacturers in discrimination and asbestos cases. Most
discrimination and asbestos-related lawsuits never go to
trial. Many are settled out of court long before a trial
begins. A number of others are settled during the trial
process for a large or small sum, depending on how the
wind blew, either for or against the defendant. Her
experience was exclusively in federal courts where civil
motions are handled by memoranda and declarations, not
by appearing in court. She also did mediations. Abel met
her shortly before she became a judge. She had mediated an
employment discrimination case. He was told that despite
her background she could be fair. After the case was settled
for a sum lower than he would have liked, he would never
recommend her to another plaintiff's attorney. She had
clerked for a Supreme Court judge, was a member of many
legal associations, and she was once a partner in a
prestigious law firm in Harbor City. That firm's reputation
was so impeccable it never represented individuals charged
with a crime. Because she had done civil defense work, her
specialty was keeping plaintiffs out of any trial setting that
might influence a jury to award a large sum of money
against her client. She knew Civil Court Rules and Rules of
Evidence as if she studied law with various reincarnations
of Hammurabi, Solon, Lycurgus, or Oliver Wendell
Holmes. Her judicial credentials were impeccable except
for the fact that she had never tried a case, either civil or

criminal in state court. She had never held a menial job, gone hungry with no money in the bank, and never socialized with people who had less than a college degree. She was short, had brown hair, and wore a constant scowl. She believed that when in doubt, it was better to trust those who appeared to have no stake in the matter, such as prosecutors and court-appointed experts.

When Abel arrived at the courtroom, Denise and Roberta were already seated on the front row of the gallery for the public. The public gallery and the lawyers' areas were separated by an old railing with a swinging door. In the area for lawyers, Culpepper and Blount were seated close together at one table. Blount greeted Abel with a two-page declaration of Linda Garvey. It denied all the allegations made by Lori Black and denounced Abel as a lawyer who obviously put winning at any cost above the health and safety of the small children. Lori Black's declaration read:

Declaration of Lori Black

I, Lori Black, do hereby declare under penalty of perjury that I am over the age of eighteen and competent to testify. I have worked for the Korean Women's Association known as the KWA for eight (8) years. For several months I was assigned as the residential home care provider for Linda Garvey. I am very concerned about the way she treats Randy and Baily Jarad. Shortly after I started work for her, she told me that the other caregivers had shared their paychecks with her. I told her that I would not give her a share of my paycheck. She stated this often and warned me if I refused to give her part of my paycheck, she would report me as having stolen from her. Eventually she did when I refused to give her part of my pay.

At first, she would not let me clean or cook. She told me white people don't know how to do those things. Finally, though, she allowed me to clean and cook, but she always criticized my work. None of my other clients have ever complained. She increased the pressure on me to give her a share of my paycheck. She wanted half. I told my supervisor that I wanted another placement. I was concerned that she would accuse me of stealing. She had done that with other caregivers. She would make remarks that money was missing, and she claimed that everyone stole from her. After I quit, Linda Garvey did accuse me of stealing from her. KWA is a bonded agency, and I understand that she has received reimbursement for money or objects that she claims were stolen from her by other caregivers. I am very concerned about the way she treats the boys. She spoils the younger boy, Baily. He always sleeps with her. She berates the older boy, Randy, all the time. She tells him that he has molested his younger brother, and she is going to send him away. She tells others when he is in the room that he lies and steals, gets in trouble at school, and has molested his brother on two occasions. When he is on time-out, he is made to sit against a wall. One time he sat for eight hours and another time for six hours. When he is on time-out, he must eat sitting against the wall. One time he dropped his plate while eating, and Linda told him that he was done eating. She tells both the boys that they are to say nothing about what happens in her house.

Linda told me that Randy was hit on the arm by a friend of hers who she calls her niece. I came to work in the morning, and she told me that her niece had beat him with a hanger. Randy had marks on his arm, and he was told not to say how it happened. On another day, I was there when Linda Garvey took Randy into the bathroom and slapped him several times. I heard him yelling and crying, and I heard her cussing at him. She buys clothes for the boys from Boosters who are people who steal. She claims that she has no money, and she has the boys steal drinks for her from soda dispensers. She told me that all the SSI money was frozen because of this case, and she needs a way to find money. When I met her, she told me that she was the best scam artist I would ever meet. I have provided home care for eight years and seen many people who are worse off than her who have received far fewer hours for home care. She told me that if there was a way to get *money, she would get it. She frequently has drug users come to her house. They come and she sells them some of her medication. One time she hit herself, then asked me to take her to the ER where she informed them that she was hit on the head and asked for pain medication. She was refused medication, and she was very angry. Her friend, Wendy McDonald, comes over and is high. I have seen them sitting together, and it looked like Linda was also high. Linda claims that she has cameras inside and outside the house and in the bathroom to watch Randy. She says that she does not trust him. She talks about the custody case in front of the boys. She says that Denise should never see the boys and that she dislikes Roberta. She told Randy and Baily that their father molested them. Linda tells them that they saw their father's dead body. After I quit working for her, she and another person came looking for me. They were knocking on doors trying to find out where I live. I consider her a dangerous person. She has the boys wait on her hand and foot. She has them carry her oxygen and fetch whatever it is she wants. She told me, 'What do I need you for when I have them?' My job was to provide Linda Garvey residential care. I did, however, at her request, make certain that the boys got on the school bus, and I*

picked them up at the bus stop. I would arrive at her place at about 8:30 a.m. I never saw her give the boys medication. Sometimes the little one would play outside, but most of the time they were to stay inside. I do not recall them ever having friends come over to play. She often asked me if I knew people who would sell her food stamps. It is not uncommon for people who sell their food stamps to sell them for half their value. Much of her house is just for show. She won't let he boys into her living room. They do not eat at the dinner table. They either eat at a counter, on the floor, or in their rooms. When she came to my apartment complex, she was with Wendy who was knocking on doors. I saw her drive away in her car. She claims that she lost her license to drive because Leonora Massy had too many tickets driving her car. I don't believe that is true. She is very much the manipulator. She told me that when the GAL came to visit one day, she deliberately did not take her insulin so that she would look bad and get sympathy. Later that day, the paramedics were called to see her, and she contacted the GAL to let him know that the paramedics had been there. She is often talking about the case to others when the boys are present. She frequently says the Jarads should never have gotten to visit the boys. She talked about how much she disliked doing depositions and leaves court papers lying around. Because of her talking and leaving court papers lying around, I learned who Mr. Abel is. I contacted Mr. Abel because of my concerns for the safety and well-being of the boys if they remain with Linda Garvey. Mr. Abel was very courteous to me and asked me many times if what I was saying was the truth. At no time did he ask me to exaggerate or lie.
SIGNED: LORI BLACK

"Do you still support Linda Garvey?" Abel asked Culpepper.

207

"You should have told me you were having the children see a counselor," replied Culpepper.

"I should have, but I didn't want to give Garvey an opportunity to coach the children even more than she already has."

"That you allege she has," interjected Blount.

"All rise," said the judicial assistant, taking up her position at the lower right of the judge's chair. The court reporter sat on the lower left.

As all rose to their feet, the judge hurried up to her seat. "You may be seated,' she said. She announced the name of the case and the cause number. She paused and looked to her right and to her left. "Are the parties ready to proceed?"

"Yes, Your Honor," said all three lawyers almost in unison.

"Mr. Blount has brought a motion that the Jarads be held in contempt for taking the children to an unauthorized counselor. Mr. Abel has brought a motion that the children immediately reside with Ms. Roberta Jarad based upon the allegations primarily contained in the Declaration of Lori Black."

"That is correct, Your Honor. These allegations are similar in nature to the statements provided previously by Marsha Barnes who lived with Linda Garvey in the past," began Abel.

"That will be enough," said the judge, cutting Abel off. "I will hear from you later, but this is Mr. Blount's motion. Your motion for custody came after his. I will hear from him first."

"Thank you, Your Honor," began Blount. "I have been representing Ms. Garvey pro bono and have never seen a lawyer act like Mr. Abel. He has sent me interrogatories, deposed Ms. Garvey, and sought her medical records. He has acted as if Ms. Garvey were a criminal. Now, he is accusing her of actually being a criminal."

"Sex trafficking is a crime," interjected Abel.

"Only allegations," snapped back Blount. "Allegations of a disgruntled employee who is accused of theft. Mr. Abel knows, or should know, that you do not subject children to counseling without advising the other side of what you are doing."

"Objection. They were not being counseled, merely interviewed."

"No more from you, Mr. Abel. I know what he means. I have read the file. I, too, am appalled at your clients' conduct. I only excuse it because I assume they took the children to a counselor based upon your advice. Is that true, Mr. Abel? Did you advise your clients that it was permissible to take the children to a professional without advising either Mr. Blount or Mr. Culpepper of what they were doing?"

"Your Honor should know that asking me about any communication I have had with my clients is a violation of the attorney/client confidentiality."

"I do know that."

"I take responsibility for what my clients did, but please do not ask me to violate my oath as a lawyer."

"How dare you! How dare you!" shouted the judge. Pointing to a far wall, she said, "Over there is the Creed of Professionalism for lawyers in our state. Go read it."

"It is hanging in every courtroom. I have read it."

"Read it now. If you refuse to read it, you are in contempt of court." She pointed to the wall, and Abel walked over to it. This is what he read:

Creed of Professionalism

*As a proud member of the legal profession
I endorse the following principles of civil professional
conduct, intended to
inspire and guide lawyers in the practice of law:*

- *In my dealings with lawyers, parties, witnesses, members of the bench, and court staff, I will be civil and courteous and guided by fundamental tenets of integrity and fairness.*
- *My word is my bond in my dealings with the court, with fellow counsel and with others.*
- *I will endeavor to resolve differences through cooperation and negotiation, giving due consideration to alternative dispute resolution.*
- *I will honor appointments, commitments and case schedules, and be timely in all my communications.*
- *I will design the timing, manner of service, and scheduling of hearings only for proper purposes, and never for the objective of oppressing or inconveniencing my opponent.*
- *I will conduct myself professionally during depositions, negotiations and any other interaction with opposing counsel as if I were in the presence of a judge.*
- *I will be forthright and honest in my dealings with the court, opposing counsel and others.*
- *I will be respectful of the court, the legal profession and the litigation process in my attire and in my demeanor.*
- *As an officer of the court, as an advocate and as a lawyer, I will uphold the honor and dignity of the court and of the profession of law. I will strive always to instill and encourage a respectful attitude toward the courts, the litigation process and the legal profession.*

This creed is a statement of professional aspiration adopted by the Washington State Bar Association Board of

*Governors on July 27, 2001, and does not supplant or
modify the Washington Rules of Professional Conduct.*

It took Abel a long time to read the code of
professional ethics because at each bullet point his mind
drifted away to thoughts of the Star Chamber. Like Family
law it was a court of equity-it had no jury to decide the
facts. The Judge was decider of the law and of the facts. If
you appealed the decision you had to hurdle over the great
deference that courts of appeal who are no more than
judges often judges who had once been trial judges give to
triers of fact. If the judge was wise all went well and if the
judge was a horse's ass things came out that way. Such
were his thoughts and the judge's patience wore thin as she
waited for him.

"Are you dawdling on purpose," she shouted.

"More unintentional than not," he replied.

When Abel returned to the front, the judge
demanded, "Did you learn anything?"

"I did."

"What would you like to tell me?"

"Many things, but best that I accept your rebuke as
a sincere effort to improve me both as lawyer and as a
human being."

The judge glared at him. " Mr. Culpepper, what
would you like to tell me? You have read the motion to
change custody and the motion to hold the Jarads in
contempt."

"I am opposed to a change of custody. Ms. Black's
accusations are disturbing, but other than her statement I
have no proof of them being true. On the other hand, Ms.
Day, the counselor that the children are seeing, is well
respected. While I deplore the methods by which the
children were taken to see her, I think those sessions should

continue. Releases should be signed, allowing all attorneys access to the records."

"Mr. Abel, your request for a change of custody is denied. The children, however, may continue to see the weekend counselor, and a release of information is to be signed so that Mr. Culpepper and Mr. Blount will have access to the records."

"Your Honor, about my request for attorney's fees and an order of contempt?" asked Blount.

"As you stated at the outset, you are acting pro bono. It pains me to say this, but since there was not a specific order that prevented taking the children to a counselor, there is no contempt. Although I do find Mr. Abel's conduct has been less than admirable. You are on the edge, Mr. Abel. On the edge," she said, with a tremble in her voice. It seemed to Abel that her constant scowl had developed into a slight frown.

"Duly noted, Your Honor. I believe that I have never acted as anything less than a zealous advocate for my client."

"I will hear no excuses," said the judge.

"I accept the Court's rebuke, will strive to do better, and to temper my actions by the Code of Professionalism to which you have directed my attention. I can assure you that as an officer of the court, as an advocate, and as a lawyer, I will uphold the honor and dignity of the court and of the profession of law. I will strive always to instill and encourage a respectful attitude toward the courts, the litigation process and the legal profession."

"Pity his memory is not as good as his conduct," interjected Blount. He received a glare from the judge for his trouble.

"In my newfound education, I will endeavor to resolve differences through cooperation and agreement of the parties that none of them will beat the children with clothes hangers, sell drugs, or engage in sex trafficking."

"That is an insult to the Court!" burst out Blount, his face suddenly turning crimson. "There has been no finding of any of those outrageous accusations."

"I am merely suggesting mutual restraints without a finding by the Court," replied Abel.

"I have not found that any of those activities by anyone has happened," said Culpepper.

"In my request, I am being civil and courteous and guided by the fundamental tenets of integrity and fairness," said Abel. "I ask that the restraints be mutual. What could be more fair than that?"

"Motion denied," said the judge. "I don't see it as necessary, and I do not think it accomplishes anything."

"Thank you, Your Honor. I must agree that such a restraint might be disregarded."

"I did not say that, nor did I imply it," said the judge. "This hearing is adjourned."

Turning away from the bench, Abel saw his clients, Roberta and Denise. Their faces reminded him of Melpomene, the Greek mask of tragedy. Linda Garvey sat on the other side of the courtroom with her eyes focused on Abel, making sure he saw that her smile was as pronounced as Thalia the muse of comedy.

23

The prospective client had rescheduled a couple times and then called to say he would be a little late. Abel responded that he had no problem staying late, that he had work to do and to arrive as soon as he could. Much of what Lori Black had related to him surprised him, but he was even more surprised by Judge Nightingale's indifference to the allegations. She seemed more concerned about the petty proprieties going on inside her courtroom than the far greater improprieties going on outside of it. He had written several pages asking the judge to reconsider her ruling and lost track of time when he thought he heard a knock at his front door but when he opened the door no one was there.

He closed the Jarad file on his laptop. His brief on the ignorance and arrogance of the judge, as enjoyable as it was to write, was simply not suitable for persuading the judge to reconsider her ruling. He opened the folder where he kept the articles he sent to the local bar magazine. Years Years ago, poet Marvin Bell had advised him that when in doubt, use the fewest words possible to express an idea. He had worked and worked on the article and thought that he had said all that he had to say on the topic he had chosen.

Curiosity is Expressed in More Ways Than in Words

"Curiosity is one of the permanent and certain characteristics of a vigorous intellect."
Johnson: Rambler #103 (March 12, 1751)

All too often we confuse verbal skills with intellect. One of the books I often refer to is the Diagnostic and Statistical Manual of Mental Disorders. It is in its Fifth edition now. The first edition I bought as a lawyer was the Third edition. With each version the list of mental illness grows, but people seem much as they were when I started out thirty years ago.

It is a helpful reference for criminal family and personal injury work. The DSM 5 diagnosis is primarily based on behavior. The check list of behaviors associated with a mental illness can make for an interesting cross examination of a psychologist whose diagnosis does not match up with the person's reported behavior. I have familiarity with the book, but am careful to not confuse my occasional ability to pronounce a word correctly with a working knowledge of psychology. Another book I refer to from time to time is "Techniques of Crime Scene Investigation," by Barry A.J. Fisher and David Fisher. It is now in its eight edition. It is useful not only for the information it imparts, but, also, as a guide to more in-depth books on particular topics such as blood splatter, and DNA. Books are like water buoys, they can point you in the right direction, but often do not tell what possible cross currents and hazards lie underneath. A crime technician demonstrated this to me one day in open court by demolishing a line of questions I had created, developed from various source books.

The Math on Trial CLE that Nigel Malden gave was had the latest crowd of any CLE put on to date by the Friends of the Library. A second Math on Trial CLE will be scheduled for some time in November. the one hour CLE will be at the City County Building. The donation requested is only fifteen dollars. Sandwiches and cookies are provided and there will be a drawing for the book Math on

Trial. You must be here to win. The book and the CLE
presented examples of smart lawyers armed with a small
amount of knowledge making major mistakes.

   Alex Trebek suggested once that writers, teachers
and lawyers as a group did well on Jeopardy because they
shared the common trait of Curiosity. Many of the lawyers
I know are always learning new things whether it be a
deeper knowledge about their particular filed of interest, or
in other matters.

   This could perhaps be a Jeopardy question- This
Roman building material is considered by many most
durable of building materials. The answer/ question is
"What is concrete," would be the Jeopardy question if that
was a Jeopardy question. The principles of underwater
construction were well known to Roman builders. Roman
concrete is far more durable than modern concrete.
Modern concrete when exposed to saltwater deteriorates
within decades, Roman concrete does not. I remembered
that as I was on my way to Home Depot buy some concrete
to put in a mailbox post. I compared that to my absolutely
useless knowledge about modern concrete. I, also, realized
that I would have far greater problems than soggy mail if
saltwater ever reached my mailbox. Fortunately, my
neighbor, whose wife was tired of looking at my old
mailbox, does know a thing or two about concrete.

   One of the most common complaints of pro see
litigants is that they are not respected by the courts.
Lawyers, on the other hand, who are opposed by a person
representing him or herself, often complain That judges
grant continuances to a pro se that would never be granted
to a lawyer. When I speak to people representing
themselves, I often ask them what they do for a trade. Often
they are in the building trade. I tell them of my limited skills

and repeated trips to hardware stores to complete a simple project.

The mailbox installation took five trips. 1. Purchase of the box, post, bracket and super quick drying cement. 2. Return of the bracket because the post came with one. 3. Return of the supper quick drying cement because it's ten second drying time was just unreasonable. 4. Purchase of two hour drying cement. 5. Purchase of additional cement because I had not bought enough. 6. Return of the bag I did not use. I wish I could say this was unusual, but it was not. Knowing this, my aim was to die before the mail box was replaced. However, my neighbor's wife wanted the box removed and found a ready support for the idea with my wife, who for the past five years had been suggesting we needed a new box.

Many of the books on how to litigate your own case read like instructions on how to make a watch, when all the person wants to know is what the time is. Fortunately, the the Neighborhood Legal Clinic offered by Tacoma Pro Bono meets the first three Mondays of every month from 6:00-8:00pm to assist those who must litigate on their own case. I say "must" because few ever really want to be their own lawyer.

I recently took a tour of workshop where church organs are made from scratch. The wood is fashioned, the metal for the pipes created and hammered into shape. My mailbox experience had all ready left me humble, but this brought me even more face to face with my limitations.

Lawyers have certain skills, but we should not confuse our book skills, writing skills and ability to turn a phrase from time to time into a winning argument with more than what they are. As lawyers, we can provide justice to those who have been wronged, and from time to time leave divided parents united in caring for their

217

children, even though they no longer live together. We can smooth the way for building projects and help social change, or block it if we have a mind to. We can do great things of service for others with our words, but those who work with their hands or travel to places we have never been or create experiment displays as vigorously as any intellectual found in our court files. Perhaps more so because they put their bodies on the line for their beliefs, while all we do is read about what others have done and compose an argument. Sometimes the inability to hire a lawyer simply comes down to who cleans out the bank accounts first. We simply must not judge a case by the inability of a person to hire a lawyer.

He attached the article to an email sent to the editor with the simple message that she was free to edit it as she thought fit. Again, he thought he heard a knock. This time on his back door, but when he went there the back porch was empty.

He went back to the article and began to wonder if he should include a paragraph or two about his struggles in shop class to build a sheet metal box that would hold water. Eventually he had, but the beads of solder weighed almost as much as the box itself. Was it worth including, did it add to the story? He pondered and looked for a possible place to include another example of his mechanical frailties. He thought some times that crows knew more about the use of tools than he did.

Again there was knock on the door. It was a loud knock. No mistaking it for the wind or a dog or raccoon. He called out that he was coming, but his thoughts were on his article and how it needed to be rewritten. He looked at his watch. Two hours had gone by that seemed like two minutes. That was the way it was when he was writing. He felt like he was outside of time. How was it that words and rhythms so entranced him? He could spend hours trying to decide if one sentence should follow another or if a comma was in the right place. He had forgotten that he had stayed late because a new client had wanted to with him. He wondered if Washington would appreciate the article. He had wanted to praise people who represent themselves. He thought of Lori Black risking her employment with the Korean Woman's Association. Would they blacklist her from other caregiver positions. Again, there was knock at the door. How long had he sat motionless, he did not know.

He rose up and smoothed the front of his shirttail. *I really should get a sign to enter or a doorbell*, thought Abel. As he walked the few short steps to the front door his mind was on his brief to the Judge Nightingale, asking her to reconsider her denial of granting Roberta immediate custody. Perhaps he thought it would be best not to say "That he learned that she cared more about decorum in her courtroom than the crimes outside her door." He liked the sentence but thought in a brief not so wise to piss off the one he wanted to persuade. Better perhaps to save it for an article or short story.

He was reaching for the doorknob when the door was slammed back at him. But for his front foot, the door would have broken his nose. The attacker was wearing a black balaclava and leather gloves. Abel staggered backwards as a fist launched at his left temple. He ducked and charged at the man who was quickly moving toward him. The man launched several swings above Abel's head as if baffled at Abel's charge and then adjusted his swings and went after Abel's body and chin. The man was taller than Abel. Abel deflected a left toward his chin with his forearm but he couldn't stop a blow to his lower ribs, sending a spasm across his chest crushing the air out of his lungs.

He moved backwards trying to get separated from the attack. But the man quickly closed the distance and pummeled him mostly with his right hooks. The man also landed several left hooks from different angles. Abel's body received a few hits, but he blocked the shots to his head with his forearms. Abel turned to escape from the small entry area, but the larger man tripped him and Abel fell face down. The attacker began kicking and stomping him on his legs and hips. The attacker was as relentless as a machine and as mute. He stomped the back of Abel's legs and began kicking Abel in the ribs. As best he could, Abel tried to protect his head with his left arm. He rose up slightly from the floor and reached across his body for his gun. He thought that he felt the gun's grip, but it wouldn't move. He wondered if he was paralyzed, but if he was paralyzed, why did he feel the kicks? He remembered the holster's trigger guard. He cleared the guard with his thumb and drew the gun while rolling onto his back. He fired a shot into the man's foot as it was coming down on him.

The man screamed and staggered backwards. Yelling and cursing, he backed out of the door hopping on one foot.

Abel staggered to his feet. Each breath sent jolts of pain until he could control his breathing. He went to the front door and heard a car engine rev and saw a car race away.

Inside his head was a hum as if he were in a beehive. He locked the front door and looked around the room. He was seeing double, and he wasn't certain what was an illusion and what was real. He was afraid to fall asleep. The harsh lights in his office were unyielding. The fluorescent hum of the overhead lights sounded like a jet engine taking off. He found his phone and called Billie for help. When they got to the hospital, he didn't have to wait to be seen. They thought the blood that covered him was his blood until they had cut away his shirt. Just before he lost consciousness he thanked the nurses for their work and apologized for taking up their time just as his grandmother had taught him to do many years ago.

<u>24</u>

On the second day, the hum in Abel's head became the buzz of an overworked transformer. On the third day, the buzz disappeared along with his double vision. He was watching an episode of *Columbo* when Father Martin dropped by the hospital to see how he was doing. "If you've come by to deliver the last rites don't bother. I'm feeling rather spry," chuckled Abel.

"I'll have to check with the Bishop to see if I can give a lawyer last rites. Your Catholic upbringing is showing. The church rejects the term 'last rites,' as inaccurate. It is not reserved for terminally ill or mortally injured people like it is in the Catholic Church and some Protestant denominations. I could give you unction. Judging by your bruises you certainly are entitled."

"Maybe another day, but I do appreciate you coming by. I'm really feeling fine except when I sneeze."

"Sneeze?"

"I have a couple of broken ribs. I asked the doctor why he didn't wrap them up the way they do in action movies. He said the pain would keep me from moving around too much. He was right."

"But you are going to be alright?"

Abel nodded and switched off the TV. "I know how it ends."

"With *Columbo*, don't you usually know who the murderer is and that he or she will be caught?"

"True, but aside from the interplay of Colombo with the murderer and his one last question, I enjoy how he figures it out. You see how the murder is done, but the clues for the capturer is right before you, yet it's usually a surprise. It is the rare mystery that is worth seeing more than once, but many of his are. In this one Robert Conrad is the killer."

"That is the one where Columbo figures out how the murder was done by how the victim's shoes are tied."

"Exactly," nodded Abel with a wince.

"Is your wife coming by. I'd like to meet her?"

"She is at the office. A friend is installing a CCTV for the front porch. So I will know who I am opening the door for."

"Isn't that a little late."

"That's what I said," Abel sighed and paid for his sigh with a wince.

"Roberta came by, and she is worried that you're going to send her a whopping bill. She said that you haven't sent her a bill after she paid her retainer. She said that she wants to pay you for what you've done. She's just worried about what the final bill will be."

"She is a good person and doing the best she can to save the boys. She shouldn't worry. I doubt that I will send her another bill."

"Can I tell her that?"

"No, no. If word gets out about what a soft touch I am, I will never get any rest."

"I read that book you recommended, *The Spirituality of Imperfection*. I enjoyed it."

"I like the idea that anything worth doing is worth doing poorly," said Abel.

"So do I," said the priest.

They talked for a while about the book. They would have talked longer, but Father Martin excused himself when a police officer entered the room to take Abel's statement.

"I am Detective Elizabeth Knight. We have met before," said the police officer. She had short brown hair and wore brown polyester slacks and a jacket outfit. A standard issue Glock 9mm was on her right hip, her badge on her belt. She was about forty and had a serious look about her, suggesting that her call was strictly professional and not out of some general concern for Abel's welfare.

Abel and she had met years ago when he was representing a college student accused of killing a drifter in a park. The case had been dismissed before it went to trial. Knight's advancement had stalled for a few years, but gained momentum when Detective Steve McCoy had taken her under his wing and taught her the fine art of writing incident reports that left out exculpatory statements, and putting definitive statements of guilt in.

"Tell me what happened."

"I gave a statement to an officer when I came into the ER."

"It was a rather disjointed statement. Somehow or other you called your wife who drove you to the emergency room. You stumbled into the waiting room, and politely asked if you could see a doctor. Then you vomited onto the receptionist's desk."

"My grandmother raised me to be polite," said Abel. "If I haven't already, please tell the receptionist I'm sorry."

"I don't relay messages, but when you're discharged, you can tell her."

"Of course."

"We have been to your office. It is sealed up as a crime scene, but you can return to it tomorrow."

"I should be released in the morning."

"What do you remember? What stands out in your mind?"

"I remember being wheeled down a hall to have my head scanned. My wife, Billie, was walking beside me. She was called to the hospital. The aide kept saying that she was not allowed to go with me. I finally told him that I hadn't won an argument with her yet, and he should give it up. He did."

"I was hoping for information about the crime, not a family moment. Did the man who attacked you say anything?"

"No. I opened the door, and he started hitting me." Abel held up his right and left forearms. They were mottled with blue and yellow bruises. "I blocked most of his blows, but some got more past me. When he hit me in the ribs, I was in pain and short of breath. I went to the ground, and he began kicking me on the legs and ribs. He went for my head as well, but I had it covered. I was lucky he was wearing soft toed shoes. Had he been wearing shit kickers I would be dead. I was face down on the ground. I found my gun I rolled over, drew my gun, and fired to stop his assault."

"You were in your office and had a gun on your person?"

"Yes. I recently acquired the cross draw holster at the recommendation of a friend."

"Were you expecting trouble? Had someone threatened you?"

"No, no threats. I have no idea who or why I was attacked."

"It just seems odd that you had a gun on you if no one had threatened you."

Abel shrugged. "You carry a gun. Has someone threatened you?"

"I am a police officer."

"I have a concealed carry permit, and I was in my office. I think it fortunate that I had a gun."

"You shot an unarmed man."

"I have no idea if he was armed or not."

"Did you see a gun?"

"I was rather busy seeing fists and stars."

"You have no idea who he was?"

"A man called me to make an appointment at the time that the man appeared at my door. He said that he was Ben or Benjamin Dawkins. I doubt he gave me his real name, though. He didn't leave a number."

"Where did you shoot him?"

"In my office."

"Don't play cute."

"I assume that I shot him in the foot. It was the closest bodily part to me."

"You didn't tell him that you had a gun? You just shot?"

"That is right. I shot him. I have defensive wounds from the top of my head to the bottom of my feet, and I shot him."

"Why didn't you just pull out the gun before he attacked you?"

"He was on me before I knew what was happening. I wish that I had shot him sooner, but in the heat of the moment I forgot that I had the gun until I rolled onto it. Pulling out a gun in the middle of a fight is not something I'm trained for. Why don't you ask him when you find him why he attacked me? From the blood and the way he backed away, I know that I shot him. Hospitals and doctors have to report gunshot wounds. I suggest you locate him. He may be able to answer the questions that I don't have answers to."

"You could have killed him. Have you thought about that? That may be why no hospital has reported him. Or he may have connections and knows a doctor who doesn't make a report. What kind of criminal has connections with criminal doctors? You may be in danger.

A criminal defense lawyer with a gun and an unknown suspect. You can see how that raises questions. Laconia Jones may be your friend, but there are unanswered questions that need to be explored. How are you and your wife doing? Any problems?"

"We are done," said Abel. "I'd know if she wanted me dead." He started to laugh, but the sharp pain of his cracked ribs prevented him from laughing.

"You must have a suspicion of who attacked you."

"Sorry. No."

"Are you just some guy who carries a gun and dreams about being Rambo?"

"I know that it takes no courage to carry a concealed weapon when nobody knows you have it

"If you withhold evidence, I could charge you with obstruction of justice."

"If it comes down to threatening a lawyer with the law, you've already lost, officer." Abel turned the TV back on. It was a *Columbo* marathon. The episode playing was "Any Old Port in a Storm. *"* "This is a fan favorite," said Abel. "It is remarkable how much Columbo gets out of suspects by being polite. You should try it some time."

"Maybe you are thinking that you'll track him down and exact revenge. Is that why you aren't telling me who attacked you?"

"I have no need of revenge. I already shot him once." He turned the volume up, and then turned it down for a moment. "Whoever attacked me had to get medical treatment. I suspect that he went to a clinic, not to a hospital. Hospitals have to report gunshot wounds. If the shooter went to a clinic, then perhaps his wife said it was an accidental shooting."

"Why would they believe a wife?"

"Maybe the wife is a police officer. If she were, you shouldn't blame her for protecting her husband."

"You got a name for me?" Knight asked.

"Leave the wife out of it if you can."

"I want the person who shot you." Knight pressed

"The only person I know who might have had a grudge against me with some boxing skills is Benis Dalton. But, I have no idea why he would come after me now. I have seen him wearing causal sneakers with wide white sides and brown leather upper. Ecco makes them, but so do other manufacturers. I may have seen white and brown when the man was kicking me. Were traces of sneakers found at my office?"

"I can't tell you that,"

"Fair enough, but my guess is that if you find those shoes of his you will find that one has a hole in it" He turned the volume back up.

Knight left as the introductory credits were ending.

Laconia came by at the end of the episode in which the murderer and Columbo are enjoying a glass of wine before the murderer gets sent to a place where fine wine is never served. "Elizabeth is not happy with you," Laconia said by way of greeting.

"I tried," said Abel, turning the TV off. "Yesterday was a *Matlock* marathon. I hope to miss whatever the marathon du jour of tomorrow is. However, at least with the old shows the actors speak so you can understand them."

"Perhaps you should adjust your hearing aid more often."

" Don't make me laugh. It's painful. If you've just come here to insult me, you can leave."

"You really have no idea who paid you a visit?"

"When McCoy and you spoke to Dalton, did either of you mention my name?"

"No, and I haven't shared the incident report with your name in it with the prosecutor. It's not in the system."

"Then, no, I have no idea who attacked me. My money was on Dalton only because I've seen the YMCA video showing that he attacked Levi." Abel paused. "And the man who made the appointment with me said he was a friend of Levi's. I just thought of that. Perhaps it was him. I am fairly certain he trashed Levi's trailer, van, and storage unit."

"Who is Levi?"

"He is the client of mine who Dalton punched in the YMCA parking lot. I told you about him."

Laconia nodded. "McCoy and I were careful not to mention your name."

An attractive nurse with no wedding band stepped into the room and asked Abel if he needed anything. Then she introduced herself to Laconia. He smiled and promised that if Abel got out of line, he'd come arrest him. Before she left the room, Laconia gave her his number, and she promised to call him. "You would be carrying my coffin and hitting on women. I bet you would drop it if you saw someone you wanted."

"Nonsense," said Laconia. "I'd carefully set your coffin down out of respect."

"For the living, not the dead."

"Respect is where you find it," laughed Laconia. "I followed up on the lead you gave us about Dalton, and it didn't go far. We tracked down the woman with the two kids. She is the guardian of the boys. She confirmed that Silas Smith was the aggressor, and Dalton had pulled his punches. Sorry things are not looking good for Riley."

"What is this woman's name?"

"That is not something you are supposed to know."

"When you talked to her, did she complain about a caregiver stealing from her?"

"Maybe. What is that to you?"

"I don't buy that Dalton would ever pull his punches. Once his rage takes over, he can't control himself. The man who attacked me was slightly under control until I fought back, then he was like a hurricane. Is the woman's name Linda Garvey?"

Laconia nodded and said, "I'm listening."

25

The case against Garvey for the murder of Silas Smith
came together quickly once forensics made a match
between the debris and DNA found on the bat with Silas
Smith's DNA. the wood fiber the bat found his scalp and
hair proved that Smith hadn't been hit by the bat. Within a
a few hours of learning about the evidence, Laconia
interviewed Randy about his bat and when he had lost it
and that Garvey had thrown it away. Randy volunteered
the day before Mamma Garvey had thrown away the bat
man with colorful clothes had come to dinner. He even
remembered that Mama Garvey had gone out the door with
his toy bat in her hand after the man had left. Not expecting
much, but in an effort to test all leads, Laconia had
contacted Child Protective Services. He learned of Silas'
call to the agency on the morning that he died, complaining
about Garvey being a money grubber who didn't care about
the children in her custody. When he took the evidence to
Eunnie to review she quickly realized that Laconia had laid
a case for murder-the motive was money. She Opportunity-
the night of the dinner: The Method was the small bat: and,
there was Evidence- the debris with DNA, and the injury
consistent with a blow to the head. As she wrote out the
declaration of probable cause, Eunnie was also writing
down the talking points for the closing argument she
planned on using at the trial, if it went that far.

Garvey and Dalton were arraigned on the same
afternoon criminal docket: Garvey for murder of Silas
Smith and Dalton for the assault of Abel. Silas, because of
his colorful clothes and notoriety in the community,

deserved to have the news camera crews in the gallery. Taking up the front row with their lenses close to the plexiglass barrier were several cameramen from local news stations.

Abel's assault was hardly newsworthy, except he was a lawyer. But the way he defended himself made it of marginal interest to those who decide what to feature on the news. If only Dalton was to be arraigned, the camera crews would not have been in the courthouse, but elsewhere filming potholes, the opening of a new sandwich shop, or whatever was needed to fill in the hour of local news time before the network news took over. Several African American men in suits and white shirts were seated in the second row behind the cameras. Each of them wore a red bow tie similar to what Elijah Muhammad frequently, if not always, wore.

Abel slipped into the back row where Sheri Dalton was seated. Court had not yet started. He recognized Dalton's wife from when he had defended Levi Yabroff. On the left side of her face and under her left eye was an extra layer of makeup. "How's your husband's foot?" asked Abel.

"I'm not supposed to talk to you," she hissed back.

"He's lucky. The gun I shot him with was a .357, but I had only loaded it with .38 ammunition."

"I will let him know you're sorry."

"I didn't say I was sorry. Hollow points do enough damage."

She nodded, "That they do, allegedly." She grinned slightly. "Those brothers up there think he is one of them."

"He's not?"

"He just pretended to be one because he wanted to sell a few houses. Lately, he has been working on angles with the Methodists. There's more money to be made from

Protestants, he says. Where once our bookshelves were filled with Black Muslim literature now sit works of John Wesley, Martin Luther and so."

On the other side of the plexiglass, the courtroom was filling with lawyers, and the judicial assistant was checking the court docket with the regular courtroom deputy.

"Officer Knight told me that you asked, if possible, she not charge me with rendering criminal assistance for getting him admitted to a clinic. Why did you do that?"

"I know you have children. He is going to do some time. Job opportunities for felons are limited. Even if he can get back into selling houses, some clients may balk at working with a felon. I wanted you to know that I can be trusted."

"Why?"

"When a person pleads to a crime, they can agree to pay restitution for an uncharged crime. When he pleas guilty, and he will plea guilty, I want him to agree to pay restitution to Levi Yabroff for the damage to his trailer, storage unit and van. The DNA evidence convicts him."

"Why would he do that?"

"It would make me happy, and prosecutors are happy when the victims are happy."

"All rise," said the judicial assistant as the judge quickly took the bench. He was in his fifties and had already been a judge for ten years. He was known for being polite and businesslike. When he was the judge in drug court, he always praised those who succeeded and gave high-end sentences to those who failed.

"Please be seated," the judge said. " Is the State ready?"

"We are, Your Honor," said Eunnie Hong. Because it was a murder case with camera crews in the gallery, she had come down to handle the arraignment. Crimes of notoriety were seldom left to an inexperienced prosecutor. "The first case is *State v Linda Garvey*," she said, and she read the case number and the charge which was First-Degree Murder.

Garvey entered the courtroom. Ignoring the guard's order not to look at the gallery, she glared at them as she walked to the defendant's table. A public defender was waiting for her there. His sole duty was to enter pleas of not guilty and ask for a lower bail than that requested by the prosecutor. Once a bail is set after lower bail has been argued for, it is difficult to get it lowered.

Eunnie stated the charges and summarized the declaration of probable cause. "The accused invited the victim to her place to discuss her continued custody of two children. He was opposed to her custody. After dinner she followed and struck him."

"Was he found where he was struck?" asked the judge, scanning the declaration.

"No, the victim suffered a subdural hematoma that worsened overnight, and he collapsed at a bus stop the next day."

"As I recall, the State charged another man with the death of Silas Smith. I believe you told me that the evidence was overwhelming."

"I thought it was, but our investigation later showed that Mr. Sean Riley had not injured Mr. Smith as believed. Charges against him have been dismissed."

"Not good to have more than one person charged with a person's murder."

"Not good at all. Our office strives for justice. When it was determined that Mr. Riley was not culpable for Mr. Silas' death, the State dismissed the charges on its own motion." Pausing to take a breath, Eunnie added, "The bat that was used by the defendant has Silas Smith's DNA on it. We have confirmed that the defendant attempted to throw the bat away the morning after she attacked Mr. Smith, but thanks to a caregiver's concern for a small child, the bat was retrieved and preserved as evidence."

"I have read the declaration of probable cause, and I am convinced that there are grounds to proceed. I find probable cause. How does the defendant plead, guilty or not guilty?"

"Your Honor, I want to be heard. I have never met this man to my left. He told me that he is my lawyer. How can he be my lawyer if I've never met him?"

"He is here for the arraignment only. How do you plead, guilty or not guilty?"

"I am the de facto parent to Randy and Baily Jarad with all rights and responsibilities derived from consideration of the court. Roberta Jarad was awarded third-party custody of the children because I have been wrongly accused and incarcerated like I was a criminal. I am upset due to the manipulation and harassment of the court-appointed officers for failing to abide by a court order to include and consult me in the transition of these children. The rife in the lives of these children and myself is a catastrophe. I am ashamed of these adults who are supposed to have the children's best interests at heart. These people have violated my rights as the de facto parent, slandering my name, making false allegations, and using the court to carry out their evil deeds. I am begging the Court to investigate the mistreatment of the children, and how I have been treated, resulting in jeopardizing my health. My rights were violated by all parties involved, including my medical records being exposed which is against the HIPPA laws. I am asking the Court for some relief in this situation. I am looking for help and answers from all parties involved to understand where everything fell apart. I am asking the Court to fix what was broken. This toy bat that I am accused of hitting poor Mr. Silas with was given to the police by John Abel. He is the very lawyer who has been behind the taking of the children from my care. The bat was a toy. How can anyone hurt a person with a toy bat?"

The judge nodded sympathetically. "All questions and those issues may be raised at a later date. But the question now is, do you plead guilty or not guilty?"

"Not guilty!" she shouted. "Not guilty!" she repeated, turning toward the cameras. "Not guilty! The person you should be charging with poor Mr. Silas' death is Benis Dalton. He's the one who beat Mr. Silas up. He beat him badly in the People's Park. I felt so sorry for Mr. Silas that I asked him to come for dinner. He was hurting and fretful when he was at my house. I even walked him home. He was unsteady on his feet. It was Benis Dalton who sacked poor Mr. Silas. Not me."

"Ms. Hong, have you heard of this accusation before?"

"There was an altercation in the park between the victim and Benis Dalton. Previously, the defendant stated that Dalton did not strike Mr. Smith. She said he was in fine shape when he came to her house for dinner."

"I lied!" yelled Garvey. "I was threatened by Dalton. He told me to say those things, or he would beat me up and toss my body in the bay. He knows violent men," she said, pointing to the row of brothers. "They wear suits and bow ties, but they are evil. They are not even Christians. I am a Christian woman who took in children abandoned by their mother, and this is the fate I must endure for my kindness."

236

"We have investigated the case and are certain that she is responsible for Mr. Smith's death."

"Please control yourself," said the judge. "A plea of not guilty has been entered. Does the State have a recommendation for bail?"

"Half a million," Eunnie responded. "She obviously has no sense of control."

"I should be allowed to go home and stay with the children I've protected all these years."

"I'll reserve argument on the issue of bail," said the judge. He motioned for the guard to escort Garvey back to her holding cell.

The guard grabbed her arm, but she shook it off and stormed out of the room shouting, "My innocence will be proved!"

Eunnie thanked the Court, after which she quickly left the courtroom and the camera crew exited as well. A young prosecutor announced that the next defendant on the docket was Benis Dalton.

Dalton limped into the courtroom, nodding to his supporters in the second row.

"The defendant is charged with first-degree assault of John Abel, a local lawyer."

"I know who he is," said the judge, scanning the declaration of probable cause. "I've heard people say they wanted to beat him up, but I didn't think anyone really would. It says here you stomped him while wearing tennis shoes. The declaration says he shot you in the foot and that your blood was found at the crime scene and parts of your shoes. When you were taken into custody at a clinic, your shoes were recovered. One had a hole in it and was covered in blood. Sargent Knight reported that Mr. Abel remembered that his attacker wore shoes similar to the ones we recovered from the clinic where Mr. Dalton was located. "

"Mr. Abel was hospitalized," said the prosecutor

"Serious charges," in toned the Judge. "Serious indeed. How do you plead, Mr. Dalton?"

"Not guilty," said Dalton, glaring at the judge.

"What is the State's recommendation for bail?"

"The State asks for bail of $100,000."

"My client is a respected member of the community. He has been a real estate agent for many years. His wife is a police officer. Yes, he was at a clinic being treated for a gunshot wound to his foot, but the evidence will show at trial that he was cleaning his gun and it accidentally discharged. I asked that he be released on personal recognizance. He has no prior history of criminal activity."

The prosecutor began to speak, but the judge waived for silence. "Bail will be $50,000 standard restrictions. If he lives at home, his wife is to have all firearms locked in a safe he has no access to."

Dalton limped away, nodding toward his supporters who quickly left the courtroom after he had disappeared into the holding cells.

As Dalton's supporters filed out, several asked Sheri if Abel was bothering her. To each, she "no." Before they parted, Abel gave her the names and numbers of three divorce lawyers and advised her not to bail Dalton out.

26

He had gotten the Jarad boys away from Garvey, but whether their lives had already been irreparably altered for the worse he didn't know. Lori Black coming forward hadn't convinced Culpepper that the children needed to immediately be removed from Garvey's home. Without Culpepper's support, the court refused to act and accused Abel of being uncivil. It took a murder charge to get the children away from Garvey. The blood that Dalton left behind at Abel's office would lead to his conviction, but as to what specific Abel did not know. There were simply too many cases to try and too few courtrooms. An overworked prosecutor might plead it down to a lesser charge. Perhaps Dalton might try to bargain for a sweet deal by turning on Garvey and saying that she blackmailed him into attacking him. That, of course, would put him back in the frame for the murder of Silas Smith.

Dalton must have believed that he killed Silas Smith, reasoned Abel. That was why he attacked Abel in exchange for Garvey saying he had pulled his punches. If Dalton knew that Garvey attacked Silas after he had gone to her house for dinner, he might not have attacked Abel. By giving Dalton a defense, Garvey undercut her own defense that Dalton caused Smith's death. Abel was certain that the prosecution would press for Garvey's conviction by saying she was the last to attack Silas Smith. But if being the last one to attack Smith was the murderer then Riley was back in the murder frame. He had pushed or startled Smith into falling backwards. A subdural hematoma could have been caused by the sudden movement backwards causing a weakened vessel to burst.

Lawyers look for cause and effect to establish guilt or liability. Medical science calculates that fifty percent of the subdural hematomas are idiopathic, which is "doctor speak"for they don't know what caused it.

From the similarities between what Marsha Barnes and Lori Black had told him, Abel was convinced that Garvey had abused the children and engaged in sex trafficking. The children were too traumatized to speak about what happened to them. Abel was certain that the only hope for justice for the children was for Garvey to be convicted of a crime. She may not have committed the particular crime for which she might be convicted, but given the quirks and uncertainties of criminal law, it didn't seem all that impossible to Abel. After all, Silas Smith, by Garvey's own words, was healthy and hungry when he went to her house for dinner. Now, saying she had lied to the police and that Silas had actually complained of a headache when he had dinner at his house could easily be dismissed by a jury as a self-serving lie. Had she lied for Dalton in exchange for Dalton attacking him, he did not know. He suspected she had. That seemed the most logical to him. He had experienced Dalton's rage and could not imagine him pulling his punches when he attacked Silas Smith. Would it be sorted out on Judgment Day, if there was one, he didn't know.

Garvey's involvement in the killing of Silas Smith would not have come to light except for Lori Black salvaging the bat and giving it to Abel. That kindness should seem like a miracle was a sad comment upon the human race, but that she had stood up for Randy and come to Abel and risked her job was far more noble than many would have done. Easy to talk brave when you have nothing on the line.

As for now, he was satisfied with the roll of the dice that some call justice. With all its flaws, shortcomings and reliance upon faulty memories, the arrogance of well paid experts, the best efforts of police, prosecutors, experts, criminals and lawyers to hide and misconstrue the facts, juries usually got to the truth of the matter, if as instructed, they put aside their prejudices. Good Luck with that Jack, laughed Abel. As if that were ever possible, he shrugged and texted Laconia to see if he was up for a cheeseburger at the Parkway Tavern.

The End
February 28, 2023
Tacoma, WA

About the Author

John Cain was born and raised in Eldora, Iowa. He is a lawyer in Tacoma, Washington. He lives with his wife, two dogs, and two cats. Over the years his poetry, essays, and letters to the editor have appeared in various magazines and newspapers.

He has lived in Washington State since 1979. In 1983, he graduated from the University of Puget Sound School of Law. Many criminal defendants ago, he graduated from the Iowa Writer's Workshop. He realizes now that had he spent more time trying to understand than be understood he would have benefited far more from his time at the University than he did.

After leaving the University of Iowa he had various low paying jobs with few responsibilities. On February 6, 1981, he was involved in a near fatal car accident. While he recovering he realized he had wasted his life. Why it was that he needed to be jacked upside the head to reach this simple and obvious conclusion, he has no idea, but he is grateful for the second chance on life. Being bruised, battered and stitched up was not fun, but it was one of the best things that ever happened to him. But for the accident he would not have decided to change his life.

Made in the USA
Columbia, SC
01 August 2023

21088978R00133